PENGUIN BOOKS

MR STONE AND THE K

V. S. Naipaul was born in Trinidad in 193
on a scholarship in 1950. He spent four years at University College, Oxford, and began to write, in London, in 1954. He has followed no other profession.

He is the author of *The Mystic Masseur* (1957; John Llewellyn Rhys Memorial Prize), *The Suffrage of Elvira* (1958), *Miguel Street* (1959; Somerset Maugham Award), *A House for Mr Biswas* (1961), *Mr Stone and the Knights Companion* (1963; Hawthornden Prize) and *The Mimic Men* (1967; W. H. Smith Award, 1968). *A Flag on the Island* (1967), a collection of short stories, was followed by a narrative history, *The Loss of El Dorado* (1969), and the novels *In a Free State* (1971; Booker Prize), *Guerrillas* (1975), *A Bend in the River* (1979), *The Enigma of Arrival* (1987) and *A Way in the World* (1994).

In 1960 he began to travel out of England. *The Middle Passage* (1962) records his impressions of colonial society in the West Indies and South America. *An Area of Darkness* (1964) is a reflective and semi-autobiographical account of a year in India. *The Overcrowded Barracoon* (1972) is a selection of his longer essays, and *India: A Wounded Civilization* (1977) is a more analytical study – prompted by the 1975 Emergency – of Indian attitudes. *The Return of Eva Perón* with *The Killings in Trinidad* (1980) contains studies of Argentina during the guerrilla crisis, Mobutu's Congo, and the Michael X Black Power murders. *Among the Believers: An Islamic Journey* (1981), a large-scale work, is the result of seven months' travel in 1979 and 1980 in Iran, Pakistan, Malaysia and Indonesia. *Finding the Centre* (1984) contains two personal narrative pieces about 'the process of writing. Both seek in different ways to admit the reader to that process.' *A Turn in the South* (1989) describes his journey through the Deep South of America, while his most recent book, *India: A Million Mutinies Now* (1990), is an engrossing account of the human upheavals of modern India.

In 1993 V. S. Naipaul was winner of the first David Cohen British Literature Award in recognition of a 'lifetime's achievement by a living British writer'.

V.S. NAIPAUL

MR STONE AND THE KNIGHTS COMPANION

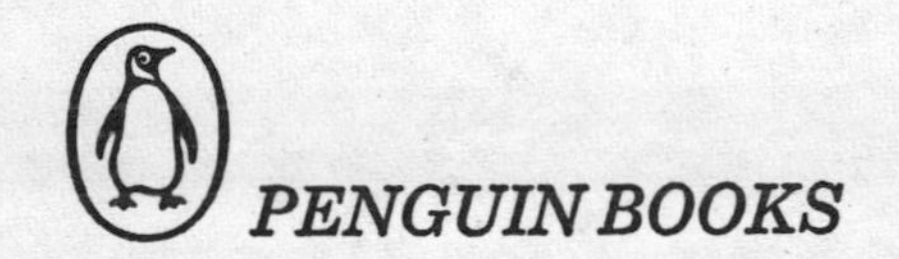

PENGUIN BOOKS

Published by the Penguin Group
Penguin Books Ltd, 27 Wrights Lane, London W8 5TZ, England
Penguin Books USA Inc., 375 Hudson Street, New York, New York 10014, USA
Penguin Books Australia Ltd, Ringwood, Victoria, Australia
Penguin Books Canada Ltd, 10 Alcorn Avenue, Toronto, Ontario, Canada M4V 3B2
Penguin Books (NZ) Ltd, 182–190 Wairau Road, Auckland 10, New Zealand

Penguin Books Ltd, Registered Offices: Harmondsworth, Middlesex, England

First published in Great Britain by André Deutsch 1963
Published in Penguin Books 1973
10 9 8 7

Set in Baskerville Monotype
Printed in England by Clays Ltd, St Ives plc

I

It was Thursday, Miss Millington's afternoon off, and Mr Stone had to let himself in. Before he could switch on the hall light, the depthless green eyes held him, and in an instant the creature, eyes alone, leapt down the steps. Mr Stone cowered against the dusty wall and shielded his head with his briefcase. The cat brushed against his legs and was out through the still open door. Mr Stone stood where he was, the latchkey in one ungloved hand, and waited for the beating of his heart, the radiation of fine pain through his body, to subside.

The cat belonged to the family next door, people who had moved into the street just five years before and were still viewed by Mr Stone with suspicion. It had come to the house as a kitten, a pet for the children; and as soon as, ceasing to chase paper and ping-pong balls and balls of string, it began to dig up Mr Stone's garden, its owners having no garden worth digging up, Mr Stone had transferred his hostility from the family to their cat. When he returned from the office he examined his flowerbeds – strips of earth between irregular areas of crazy paving – for signs of the animal's obscene scuttlings and dredgings and buryings. 'Miss Millington! Miss Millington!' he would call. 'The cat pepper!' And heavy old Miss Millington, aproned down to her ankles, would shuffle out with a large tin of pepper dust (originally small tins had been thought sufficient: the picture of the terrified cat on the label looked so convincing) and would ritually sprinkle all the flowerbeds, the affected one more than the others, as though to obscure rather than prevent the animal's activities. In time the flowerbeds had become discoloured; it was as if cement had been mixed with the earth and dusted on to the leaves and stems of plants.

Now the cat had penetrated into the house itself.

The beating of Mr Stone's heart moderated and the shooting pain receded, leaving a trail of exposed nerves, a lightness of body below the heavy Simpson's overcoat, and an urge to decisive action. Not closing the front door, turning on no lights, not taking off his overcoat or hat, depositing only his gloves and briefcase on the hall table, he went to the kitchen, where in darkness he opened the larder door and took out the cheese, still in its Sainsbury wrapping, from its accustomed place – Miss Millington shopped on Thursday mornings. He found a knife and carefully, as though preparing cocktail savouries, chopped the cheese into small cubes. These he took outside, to the front gate; and glancing about him in the sodden murk – some windows alight, no observer about – he laid a trail of cheese from gate to door, up the dark carpeted hall, now bitterly cold, and up the steps to the bathroom. Here, sitting on the cover of the lavatory bowl, still in his hat and overcoat, he waited, poker in hand. The poker was not for attack but self-defence. Often, walking down that cat-infested street, he had been surprised by a cat sitting sedately on a fence post at the level of his head, and he had always made as if to shield his face. It was a disgraceful action, but one he could never control. He feared the creatures; and there were all those stories of cornered cats, of cats growing wild and attacking men.

The damp air filled the hall and invaded the bathroom. The darkness and the silence emphasized the cold He had visions of dipping the cat's paws in boiling oil, of swinging the creature by its tail and flinging it down to the pavement below, of scalding it in boiling water. He got up from the lavatory seat and turned on the geyser. Instant hot water! The water ran cold, then after the *whoomph!* as the jets caught, lukewarm, then at last warm. The geyser needed cleaning; he must remind Miss Millington. He filled the basin and sat down again on the lavatory bowl. The water-pipes ceased to hum; silence returned.

Some minutes later, five, perhaps ten, he remembered. It was rats that ate cheese. Cats ate other things. He put on lights everywhere, closed the front door, and turned on fires.

The cheese he forgot. It was a pleasurably agitated Miss Millington who reported the next morning on the disappearance of her cheese from the larder, and its conversion into cubes laid in a wavering line from gate to bathroom. He offered no explanation.

This incident, which might be said to have led to his undoing, did not arise out of Mr Stone's passion for gardens. Gardening as he practised it was no more than a means, well suited to his age, which was sixty-two, of exhausting the spare time and energy with which his undemanding duties in one of the departments of the Excal company, his status as a bachelor and his still excellent physique amply provided him. The habit had come late to him. He relished the activity rather than the results. It mattered little to him that his blooms were discoloured by pepper dust. His delight lay more in preparing the ground for planting than in the planting, which sometimes never occurred. Once his passion had been all for digging. When this came to an end – after he had punctured a water main – he decided to hoard his refuse, to spare none for the local council. Strict instructions were given to Miss Millington; and the refuse of his household, dutifully presented by her for his daily inspection, he spread afternoon after afternoon, with a miser's delight in its accumulation, over the front garden. The following year he planted grass; but so ferociously did he mow the tender shoots – with a mower bought for the purpose – that before the end of the spring what he had thought of as his lawn had been torn to bare and ragged earth. It was after this that he had covered most of the garden with crazy paving, which proved to be a great absorber of moisture, so that even in a moderate summer his plants wilted as in a drought.

Still he persevered, finding in his activity a contented solitude and opportunity for long periods of unbroken reflection. And the incident of that evening could be said to have arisen out of his solitude, the return to a house he knew to be empty. It was in the empty house, on these occasions of Miss Millington's absence, that he found himself prey to fancies which he knew to be grotesque but which he ceaselessly indulged. He thought of moving pavements: he saw himself, overcoated and with his briefcase, standing on his private moving strip and gliding along, while walkers on either side looked in amazement. He thought of canopied streets for winter, the pavements perhaps heated by that Roman system he had seen at Bath. One fantasy was persistent. He was able to fly. He ignored traffic lights; he flew from pavement to pavement over people and cars and buses (the people flown over looking up in wonder while he floated serenely past, indifferent to their stupefaction). Seated in his armchair, he flew up and down the corridors of his office. His imagination had people behave exaggeratedly. The dour Evans trembled and stammered; Keenan's decadent spectacles fell off his face; wickedly giving Miss Menzies a wig, he had that jump off her head. Everywhere there was turmoil, while he calmly went about his business, which completed, he as calmly flew away again.

Miss Millington, returning on Friday mornings, sometimes found the fruit of her master's solitude: a rough toy house, it might be, painstakingly made from a loaf of bread which, bought on Thursday morning, was on Thursday evening still new and capable of easy modelling; the silver paper from a packet of cigarettes being flattened by every large book in the house, the pile rising so high that it was clear that the delicately balanced structure had in the end become her master's concern; objects left for her inspection, admiration and eventual dismantling, but which by an unspoken agreement of long standing neither he nor she mentioned.

That she should mention the cheese was unusual. But

so was the incident, which was, moreover, not to be buried like the others. For how often, by a person still to him unknown, was the incident of that Thursday evening to be repeated in his presence, as a funny, endearing story, to which he would always listen with a smile of self-satisfaction, though on the evening itself, in the cold darkness of the empty house, he had acted throughout with the utmost seriousness and, even on the discovery that cats did not eat cheese, had found nothing absurd in the situation.

Exactly one week later, on the twenty-first of December, Mr Stone went, as he did every year at this time, to the Tomlinsons' dinner party. He had been to teacher training college with Tony Tomlinson, and though their paths had since diverged, their friendship was thus annually renewed. Tomlinson had remained in education and was a figure of some importance in his local council. From initialling the printed or duplicated signatures of others he had risen to having other people initial his, which was now always followed by the letters T.D. On their first appearance these letters had led Mr Stone to suggest at one of these annual dinner parties that Tomlinson had become either a teacher of divinity or a doctor of theology; but the joke was not repeated the following year, for Tomlinson took his Territorial Decoration seriously.

According to Tomlinson, Mr Stone had 'gone into industry'. And it was also Tomlinson who designated Mr Stone as 'head librarian'. 'Richard Stone,' he would say. 'An old college friend. Head librarian with Excal.' The 'with' was tactful; it concealed the unimportant department of the company Mr Stone worked for. The title appealed to Mr Stone and he began using it in his official correspondence, fearfully at first, and then, encountering no opposition from the company or the department (which was in fact delighted, for the words lent a dignity to their operations), with conviction. And so, though Tomlinson's dinners had increased in severity and grandeur with the years, Mr Stone continued to be invited. To Tomlinson his presence was a pole and a comfort, a point of rest; more, it was a proof of Tomlinson's loyalty; it acknowledged, at the same time, that their present exalted positions made respectable a past which might otherwise have encouraged speculation.

The guest of honour changed from year to year, and Tomlinson in his telephone invitation always reminded Mr Stone that if he came he might make a few useful contacts. It seemed to Mr Stone that both he and Tomlinson were past the time for useful contacts. But Tomlinson, in spite of his age and an advancement which must have exceeded all his hopes, was still restless with ambition, and it amused Mr Stone to see him 'in action'. It was easy at these dinners to distinguish the 'contact'. Tomlinson stuck close to him, in his presence looked pained, sometimes distracted, as though awaiting punishment or as though, having cornered his contact, he didn't know quite what to do with him; and he spoke little, contenting himself with asking questions that required no answer or with repeating the last three or four words of the contact's sentences.

But when Mr Stone went to the dinner this year, he found that Tomlinson's word about the contact had been only a matter of habit; that there was no one to whom Tomlinson stuck close and whose words he echoed; and that the centre of attention, the leader of talk, was Mrs Springer.

Mrs Springer was over fifty, striking in her garnets, a dark red dress of watered silk, cut low, the skirt draped, and a well-preserved gold-embroidered Kashmir shawl. Her manner went contrary to her dress; it was not a masculinity she attempted, so much as an arch and studied unfemininity. Her deep voice recalled that of a celebrated actress, as did her delivery. Whenever she wished to make a telling point she jerked herself upright from the waist; and at the end of one of her little speeches she subsided as abruptly, her knees slightly apart, her bony hand falling into the sink of the skirt thus created. So that the old-fashioned jewellery and the dress, which, though of irreproachable cut, appeared to accommodate rather than fit her body, seemed quite distinct from the personality of the wearer.

She had already established herself as a wit when Mr Stone arrived. There were smiles as soon as she began to speak, and Grace Tomlinson appeared to be acting as cheer-leader. What Tomlinson did for the 'contact' in previous years, Grace was now doing for Mrs Springer who, Mr Stone learned, was her friend.

They were talking about flowers. Someone had expressed admiration for Grace's floral decorations (which, with her corsage and her dinner-party arrangements, were the result of a brief course at the Constance Spry school in St John's Wood).

'The only flower I care about,' Mrs Springer said, cutting across the muttered approvals, 'is the cauliflower.'

Grace laughed, everyone laughed encouragingly, and Mrs Springer, subsiding into her seat and seeming to rock, within her dress, on her bottom, widened her knees and briskly rearranged her skirt into the valley, a crooked smile playing about her face, emphasizing the squareness of her jaws.

So, destroying silences, hesitations, obliterating mumblings, she held them all.

The talk turned to shows lately seen. Up to this time, apart from an occasional loud *Mmm*, which could have meant anything, Tomlinson had been silent, his long thin face more pained, his eyes more worried than usual, as though without his contact he was lost. But now he sought to raise the discussion, which had already declined into an exchange of titles, to a more suitable intellectual level; this was acknowledged as his prerogative and duty. He had been, he said, to *Rififi*, had gone, as a matter of fact, on the recommendation of a person of importance.

'Extraordinary film,' he said slowly, losing nothing of his suffering appearance, looking at none of them, fixing his eyes on some point in space as though drawing thoughts and words out of that point. 'French, of course. Some things these French films do extremely well. Most extraordinary. Almost no dialogue. Gives it quite an impact, I must say. No dialogue.'

'I for one would be grateful,' Mrs Springer said, tearing into Tomlinson's reflections, which he at once abandoned, looking a little relieved. 'I hate these subtitles. I always feel I'm missing all the naughty bits. You see people waving their hands and jabbering away. Then you look at the subtitles and all you see is "Yes".' She spoke some gibberish to convey the idea of a foreign language and garrulousness. 'Then you look and you see "No".'

The observation struck Mr Stone as deliciously funny and accurate. It corresponded so exactly to his own experience. He longed to say, 'Yes, yes, *I*'ve felt like that.' But then Grace was offering sherry again and, infected by the witty mood, said when she filled Mrs Springer's glass, 'Especially for you, Margaret. Untouched by hand.'

Mrs Springer jerked herself up again. 'When you hear that anything is untouched by hand,' she said, 'you can be pretty sure it has been touched by foot.' And she took her glass to her lips, as though about to drain it.

Mr Stone sat speechless with admiration. When his own glass was being refilled he was emboldened to try one of the office jokes.

'I see,' he said, 'that you are anxious to get me under the affluence of incohol.'

There was no response. Tomlinson looked distressed, Grace pretended not to hear, Mrs Springer didn't hear. Mr Stone put his glass to his lips and sipped long and slowly. The joke wasn't even his own; it was one of Keenan's, of Accounts. People in the office pretended to groan when Keenan said it – that ought to have warned him – but Mr Stone had always thought it extremely funny. He knew that puns were in bad taste, though he didn't know exactly why. He resolved to be silent, and his resolve was strengthened when, as they were getting ready to go to the dining-room, Grace informed him, with a touch of reproof, that Mrs Springer was in fact in profound mourning, having not long before buried her second husband. This then explained Grace's solicitude, and the licence Mrs Springer appeared to enjoy. It also invested Mrs Springer with a glamour over and above her own brilliance, a glamour of which she appeared not unaware.

So far Mrs Springer had taken little notice of Mr Stone, and at dinner they were far apart, each barely perceptible to the other, in the candle-lit gloom, through the candles and flowers and the innumerable novelties in carved wood, manger scenes, pine trees, tarnished relics of an Austrian holiday which the Tomlinsons had managed to turn into their traditional decorations. On two small tables in the outer circle of gloom there were those Christmas cards, selected from the cards of more than a decade, which Grace said she couldn't bear to throw away. They were either very large or very ornate, one or two edged with lace; and every year they were thus taken out and displayed. It was this display which now held the attention of the table, of Mrs Springer and Mr Stone. And indeed for him it was a pleasure and a reassurance to enter this festive room after twelve months, to find himself in the same atmosphere and to see the same decorations.

It wasn't until after dinner, when the men joined the ladies, that Mrs Springer spoke directly to Mr Stone.

'Here,' she said flirtatiously, patting the seat beside her. 'You sit next to me.'

He did as she asked. No subject of conversation immediately presented itself, and he noticed that she had the appearance, as he had seen three or four times that evening, of someone lost in thought or of someone thinking of something to say. And before the silence became embarrassing she had spoken.

'Do you,' she asked, turning upon him with that suddenness he had begun to associate with her, 'like cats?'

'Cats,' he said. 'Well, I suppose it depends. This thing happened the other day. Just last week, as a matter of fact –'

'I think all these animal lovers talk' – she paused, and a

mischievous light came into her eyes, as it did whenever she was about to use an improper word (she had already used bitch and bloody) – 'a lot of rubbish.' She spoke these last words with a curious emphasis, as though they were in themselves witty; she made them sound like *a lotta rubbish.*

'This one attacked me the other day,' Mr Stone said. 'Attacked – '

'I'm not surprised. They're creatures of the jungle.'

'Jumped down the steps at me as soon as I opened the door. Gave me quite a fright, really. And then – it's very funny, really . . .'

He paused, not sure whether to go on. But encouragement was in her eyes. And he told the story. He told it all. He caricatured himself, finding in this a delight long forgotten. He described, with gruesome elaboration, his visions of boiling the cat in oil or water; he mentioned the turning on of the geyser, the filling of the sink, the sitting on the lavatory seat with the poker in his hand. And he held her! She listened; she was silent.

'Cheese,' she said at the end. 'You foolish man! Cheese! I must tell Grace about this.'

She made the story her own. She told it slowly and told it well. He noted her additions and ornamentations with pleasure and gratitude; and while she spoke, sitting forward and upright, he leaned back on the sofa, his broad shoulders rounded, looking down at his lap, smiling, cracking walnuts, looking up from time to time when there were exclamations, his eyes bright and gentle below his high, projecting forehead.

Thereafter she possessed him. She brought him into all her conversations. 'Cheese, Mr Stone?' she would say. Or, 'Mr Stone prefers cheese, though.' And the word always raised a laugh.

It was for him a new sensation; he luxuriated in it. And when towards the end of the evening, after the musical interlude, they again found themselves sitting side by side, and Mrs Springer said, 'Have you noticed how these walnuts look like brains?' he felt confident enough to say, loudly, 'I imagine that's why they're called nuts.'

The words hushed the room. Someone handling the crackers hesitated; then in the silence came the involuntary cracking of the nut.

'*I* think that's very funny,' Mrs Springer said.

But even she was too late to give the lead.

He left the house feeling unhappy, disgraced, dissatisfied. He was overcome by a sense of waste and futility and despair.

Mr Stone liked to think in numbers. He liked to think, 'I have been with Excal for thirty years.' He liked to think, 'I have been living in this house for twenty-four years.' He liked to think of the steady rise of his salary, since he had gone into industry, to its present £1,000 a year; and he liked to think that by earning this sum he was in the top five per cent of the country's wage-earners (he had read this fact somewhere, possibly in the *Evening Standard*). He liked to think he had known Tomlinson for forty-four years. And though it was an occasion of grief – the sharpest he had known – he liked to think that it was forty-five years since his mother had died.

His life, since his recovery from that disturbance, he saw as a period of protracted calm which, by reference to what had gone before, he had never ceased to savour in his special way. Life was something to be moved through. Experiences were not to be enjoyed at the actual moment; pleasure in them came only when they had been, as it were, docketed and put away in the file of the past, when they had become part of his 'life', his 'experience', his career. It was only then that they acquired colour, just as colour came truly to Nature only in a coloured snapshot or a painting, which annihilated colourless, distorting space. He was in the habit in odd moments of solitude of writing out neatly tabulated accounts of his career such as might have been submitted to a prospective employer; and it always was a marvel to him that the years had gone on, had rolled by so smoothly, that in spite of setbacks and alarms his life had arranged itself with a neatness and order of which the boy of seventeen had never dreamed.

Cherishing the past in this way, he cherished his appearance. He was a big man, well-made; his clothes sat well on him. The performance of a habitual action he never rushed, whether it was the putting on of a coat or the unfolding of a paper after dinner. For these two reasons he looked older than he was: there was about him the not excessive but always noticeable tidiness of the very old who are yet able to look after themselves. And he cultivated his habits. He shaved the right side of his face first; he put on his right shoe first. He was strict about his food, observing the régime he had laid down for himself as punctiliously as if it had been ordered by a trusted doctor. He read the first page and no more of the *Telegraph* at breakfast; the rest he went through at the office. He bought two evening newspapers, the *News* and the *Standard,* from a particular vendor at Victoria; without glancing at them he folded them and put them in his briefcase; they were not to be read on the train (he mentally derided those who did so), but were to be read at leisure after dinner, the news to be savoured not as news, for he instantly forgot most of what he read, but as part of a *newspaper*, something which day by day produced itself for his benefit during this after-dinner period, an insulation against the world out of which it arose.

The present was flavourless; its passing was not therefore a cause for alarm. There was a tree in the school grounds at the back of his house by which he noted the passing of time, the waxing and waning of the seasons, a tree which daily when shaving he studied, until he had known its every branch. The contemplation of this living object reassured him of the solidity of things. He had grown to regard it as part of his own life, a marker of his past, for it moved through time with him. The new leaves of spring, the hard green of summer, the naked black branches of winter, none of these things spoke of the running out of his life. They were only a reminder of the even flowing of time, of his mounting experience, his lengthening past.

All around him were such reminders of solidity, continuity and flow. There were the Christmas decorations of the Tomlinsons, each year more tarnished. In the office Miss Menzies, his assistant (over whom he was 'head librarian': the department now had no librarian proper), had exactly eighteen 'business' outfits, a variety and number that had at first stupefied him, unused though he was to noticing women's clothes, but a number which in the end had formed part of the soothing pattern of his existence. Individual outfits faded and were replaced, but the number remained constant, one outfit for each day of the week until three weeks had passed and the cycle began again. In time he had grown to recognize the days of the week from these outfits. Their passing away, their conversion into rough clothes (impossible, though, to imagine Miss Menzies in rough clothes, and uncorseted), their disintegration, as he imagined, into dusters, were like the shedding of the leaves of his tree; her new garments were like the leaves of spring.

And at home, Miss Millington. Every Thursday afternoon the old soul went to the cinema to the cheap show for pensioners; and she continued to do so even after he had bought a television set. He suspected that she slept through the films, and it always gave him pleasure on Friday morning to have her say the fiery or romantic titles. 'What was the film you saw yesterday, Miss Millington?' '*To Hell and Back*, sir,' she would say, no expression on her square, pallid face, her hoarse, indistinct voice making him think of a gasping fish.

Now, this Friday morning, shaving in the cold bathroom, he saw through the window, just beginning to stream, the familiar winter view. Beyond the bare tree were the sodden, smoking grounds of the girls' school. This portion of it, removed from the buildings and the tennis courts, was much used in summer by the very young pupils, creatures who took a delight in the feel of their companions' bodies and always in their games contrived to come together in little heaps; but now in winter it was empty except on some mornings for a hard-calved games mistress and her red-legged band. Beyond the school grounds were the backs of the two houses of people he didn't know and had mentally christened The Male (a small stringy man with a large family) and The Monster (an enormously fat woman who hibernated in winter and in the spring tripped out daintily among her flowers in what looked like a gym slip, wielding a watering can like a choric figure). The Male was always hanging out of windows, painting, sawing, hammering, running up tall ladders, making improvements to his nest. Mr Stone watched him whenever he could, hoping he would one day fall. Such frenzied home-making he detested almost as much as the sight of the men of the street cleaning their cars on a Sunday morning. He took pleasure instead in the slow decay of his own house, the time-created shabbiness of its interiors, the hard polish of old grime on the lower areas of the hall wallpaper, feeling it right that objects like houses should age with their owners and carry marks of their habitation.

But this morning the familiarity of the scene did not soothe him. He felt only a faint unease, whose origin he couldn't place and which, persisting, gave him a twinge of alarm, for it seemed that all the ordered world was threatened.

Miss Millington was downstairs, heavy, slow, too old for work, too helpless to retire, her face unhealthily pale and puffy, the small eyes watering and sleepy. Her long white apron hung over her shiny black skirt which reached down to her swollen ankles.

'What was the film you saw yesterday, Miss Millington?'

'*A Night to Remember,* sir. It was a very good film, sir. About the *Titanic.*' One of the rare comments she had volunteered on films she hadn't slept through, the *Titanic* still for her a disaster over-riding those of two wars.

In the neat tabulations of his life he had taken Miss Millington into account: she had been with him for twenty-eight years. That she must one day die had occurred to him, but it was not a thought that stayed with him for long. This morning, probing his unease, he persuaded himself, as he had never done before, that the woman before him, slowed down by age and by flesh which was bulky but not robust, was soon to die. And at once everything about the morning ritual, even as it happened, seemed to belong to the past. It was not an event which was attaching itself to his hoard of experience, but something to which he was saying good-bye.

This was a fancy, foolish as he knew most of his fancies to be. But it refused to be dispelled.

He folded the *Telegraph*, running his thumb-nail down the folds, and inserted it into his leather briefcase, which was dark in patches and shining in others, ageing well, like its owner. (He had had it for twenty-two years, and resented as an affront and a piece of trickery the advertisement he saw in the train about men 'like you' needing a new *leather* briefcase.) Then, with the putting on of the heavy Simpson's overcoat and his bowler, he was ready.

It was a time of year when routine was everywhere broken, the streets impossible, when for a whole week life was dislocated, Christmas week, with little work done, for the lonely and the unhappy tedious days to be lived through until the holidays were over and routine returned. Miss Menzies was in an outfit he recognized; she was as plumply corseted, as powdered and perfumed, as high-heeled and brisk, as 'business'-like as ever; even on this morning she managed to look occupied, though there was little to do. A letter from Sir Harry, the head of Excal, to *The Times* had to be attended to. This letter was in Sir Harry's finest vein of irony; he criticized the sluggishness of the shops in not having any Easter goods, and complained of his difficulty in making his Easter purchases because of the crowds of Christmas shoppers. The letter was a tailpiece to the correspondence he had initiated in late September, under the heading, 'The Antipodean Advance of Christmas'. A request from one of the department's 'writers' unearthed yet another of those folders which Miss Menzies's male predecessor, appointed shortly after the end of the war, had so woefully mismanaged. The man was barely literate; his idea of filing a magazine article was to tear the pages out and staple them at the top, so that consecutive reading was as difficult as it was infuriating. (In an unusual burst of anger and energy, Mr Stone had managed to have the man degraded to Stores, in the basement; and from the basement, as well as from the dingy restaurant of the nearby LCC cookery school where some of the staff had lunch for a few ill-spent pence, the man had for many years afterwards issued warnings about the imminent collapse of the department's filing system.) After the folder had been put right, there was nothing more to do. The pub, where Mr Stone went for his lunchtime glass of Guinness, was unbearably hot and overcrowded. The glasses, hastily dipped in water, were not clean. He stood in the open doorway, drinking the drink he could not relish, struggling with the new sensation of threat which he could not subdue and which was nagging him at last into an awareness of his own acute unhappiness, standing at the edge of the boisterous, beery crowd.

Shuffling that evening with the damp, steaming queue into the Underground station, to get a train to Victoria, his attention was caught by a London Transport poster. It was a new one, and had possibly been released for this midwinter's day.

In these dark damp days it is hard for us, daily pacing city pavements, to believe that winter is on the wane, that the days steadily lengthen. Below the frozen earth, however, and in the stripped black trees, life goes on. A trip to London's countryside, where the winter-dun wrapping of buds conceals all the season's muted preparation, will reassure those who doubt the coming of Spring.

Those who doubt the coming of Spring: the words magnified and gave a focus to his uneasiness. They recalled a moment – then, memory and fear quickening, he saw that they recalled several moments, which had multiplied during the last year – of unease, unsettlement: a fleeting scene in a film, a remark in the office, an item in the newspaper, one of his stray thoughts: moments he had thought buried, for they formed no part of the pattern of his life, but which now, through all the mechanical actions and unseen sights of the familiar journey home, rose revivified, one after the other, to be examined, discarded, taken up again.

And on this day of upset and disorder something else occurred which sent him scuttling home to Miss Millington in what was almost fear.

He was walking down the High Road. It was dark, the pavements in a cold sweat of mud. He was passing the dimly-lit entrance of the public library when just for a moment he saw a woman standing with a boy on the steps. Just for a moment he saw, and looked away in horror. The boy had fangs instead of teeth. And in the attitude of the woman there was all the lonely solicitude of a mother for her deformed child. A boy, with limbs like other boys! He thought of rats that must nibble to keep their teeth from transfixing their brains. He was unwilling to believe what he had just seen. He dared not look back. He carried the picture with him: the foolish face, the yellow fangs: the impulses of growth turned sour and virulent.

Seconds later he passed the well-known shop, its windows lighted and streaming. He stopped, breathed deeply, a theatrical gesture, and closed his eyes.

An old man, neat with overcoat, briefcase and hat, standing before the window of the joke-shop, seeming to smile at the imitation glasses of Guinness, the plastic faeces, the masks, the rubber spiders, the joke teeth.

Abandoning the garden to the cat, Miss Millington to her relations (he believed she had a number of grand-nieces for whom during the Thursday morning shopping she sometimes bought little gifts of sweets), and abandoning the few worn Christmas decorations which Miss Millington put up every year in the hall, the dining-room and a little way up the stairs, decorations which suggested the end rather than the beginning of a festival and which neither of them stayed to enjoy on the day, Mr Stone went to Banstead, to his widowed sister, a former schoolteacher, with whom he always spent Christmas.

He believed that his absence in Banstead over the Christmas holidays was a secret, and he did his best to keep it so. In spite of the notices on the board in front of the police station, in spite of the leaflets and advertisements, he never informed the police, for it was his conviction that they were in league with the thieves of the neighbourhood. Burglars were always on his mind when he went to visit his sister. She was harassed by them, and a good deal of her conversation was about burglaries, abortive or successful, and measures against burglaries. Her fear of burglars was one of the reasons she gave for her frequent moves. In twelve years she had moved from Balham to Brixton to Croydon to Sutton to Banstead, each move taking her farther out of the city, and though she was always up to the last minute full of plans for each house, her houses had an unfinished look, which Mr Stone could not help contrasting with the appearance of his own.

But it was always a pleasure to go to Olive's. Between Mr Stone and his sister there existed a relationship which had scarcely changed since childhood. The female attentions, over and above those provided by Miss Millington, of which he occasionally felt the need, were supplied by Olive during their brief visits to each other. And he was the man whose opinions she quoted, whose habits she studied and humoured and built stories around, whose occasional jokes she passed off as her own. The relationship had suffered during the war when suddenly, at the age of thirty-seven, Olive had married. Less than a year later Olive's husband died, and shortly afterwards Gwen was born. The relationship survived, though the birth of Gwen brought into it an element of falsity, for Mr Stone did not greatly care for children and did not care at all for Gwen. But for Olive he had grown to care more. The events of that year had marked her. Her hair went grey. Her fine teeth were destroyed; her lips, adapting themselves to their protective function, lost their shape and still after all these years suggested vulnerable gums and exposed nerves. Spittle gathered at the corners of her mouth when she spoke; her speech became slower and was sometimes slurred.

Mr Stone had, however, tried with Gwen. He knew, having heard and read it often enough, that children were like dogs: they 'knew' when adults or 'grown-ups', a word he had had to add to his vocabulary, didn't like them. He knew that the handling of children required a rare skill which was compounded of simplicity and complete honesty. And he knew that the whole tedious business was a test of the grown-up's character. He had tried. He had talked seriously to her and played games seriously with her. But he could not always gauge the level at which she was momentarily operating, and it was not infrequent for her to ask him to stop being stupid. These afternoons, 'with children', of whose relaxing charms he had heard so much, left him exhausted and occasionally with feelings that were murderous. But what fixed his distaste for the child was when, on a visit to a fairground just three years ago, she had rejected his offer to go on the big dipper because, as she said, 'I have no intention of screaming like a shop assistant on holiday.' The words came out pat, just like that; they were clearly not her own. She was thirteen then, and it had given him a deep pleasure to see her grow fat and ungainly, with those plump forearms and short, stupid fingers which always irritated him in women. Puppy fat, Olive said; but it showed no sign of melting and he did what he could to encourage it. Chocolate, for example, which Olive forbade, was effective. Gwen was inordinately fond of it and he secretly gave her half-pound bars whenever he could. Even this did not improve their relations, for she made it plain that she regarded these gifts as bribes and that her affection was too important a thing to be bartered.

Suitable gifts, though, had been another of the problems that came with the creature. The Enid Blyton stage had seemed to be going on safely for eternity; but without warning the creature's tastes changed, rendering futile and laughable the 'Five' book he had stood in a long queue in Selfridge's to get autographed by the writer, together with her personal expression of good wishes to Gwen. Once he had brought ridicule on himself by giving her a toy handbag which was suitable for a girl of eight but not for one of fifteen. Last year he had solved the problem by giving a two-pound cheque, money down the drain; this year he would do the same.

So, though he had never come to accept her as part of Olive, he accepted her as part of Olive's home. As Gwen had grown older Olive had seemed to reassert her separate identity, and he felt that the element of falsity in his relationship with his sister had diminished. Olive could still give him solace; she could still exercise his protective pity. To go to her was like going home; to get away from her was a recurring liberation.

But not even Olive could remove the unease with which he had come to her this year. She was welcoming and ministering and calm and slow as always. She wore the brown slacks he associated with her, a habit of dress dating from the war, which always inspired him with tenderness for her. She had the height and slim hips for slacks, but she wore them with such apparent disregard for her appearance that Mr Stone would have found them slightly comic if they didn't reveal her stiff-waisted walk, the upper half of her body bent forward a little, so that she always had a purposeful air, as though about to rearrange things.

The days took their usual course. On Christmas eve he helped with the decorations, enduring the snappish criticisms of Gwen. (Who were such a creature's friends? He had a vision of her, brows contracted until she was almost cross-eyed, walking down the street in her school uniform, hugging her satchel to her stomach, and chattering away between sucks on a sweet about an 'enemy' to a smaller, silent companion, who would soon become an 'enemy' as well.) Then he drank Guinness and watched television while Olive was busy in the kitchen. At meal after meal he watched Gwen, fat and sickly with unfulfilled urges, putting away sweets and potatoes with relish. Olive objected. But: 'It's Christmas,' Mr Stone said.

Of these familiar things, however, he could no longer feel himself part. They had the heightened reality, which is like unreality, that a fever gives to everyday happenings. And at last it was time to leave. He took one of Olive's puddings, as he did every year. The bowls he never returned. They remained, washed and white, in one of Miss Millington's cupboards, this year's bowl fitting into the pile of all the previous years', stacked away as neatly as his experience, his past.

He returned to see the garden freshly covered with pepper dust: Miss Millington in command of the house, the cat at it again. But what a few days before would have roused him to pleasurable anger now left him unmoved. The naked tree permitted a clear view of The Male's back window, curtained and lighted in its sickly green frame (a colour chosen by The Male last spring and applied with loving care to all the exterior woodwork of his establishment). The Monster's house was unlighted. On this evening, the mists gathering in the silent school grounds, the day dying with the feel of the death of the holiday, it seemed that the world was in abeyance.

Next morning there was a letter for him. It was from Mrs Springer. She expressed her delight at meeting him and wondered whether he would like to come to a small New Year's eve gathering. She promised biscuits and cheese, which word was followed by a mark of exclamation in parenthesis. And the letter ended, 'As you can imagine, I am trying to cheer myself up, I do hope you can make it.'

Several things about the letter irritated him. He was a purist in matters of punctuation, and Mrs Springer had used a comma where she should have used a full stop. Her attempts at wit fell flat in her sloping old-fashioned writing, which was prim and characterless. He thought the reference to the cheese, and the exclamation mark, foolish, and the reference to her mourning ostentatious and insincere.

But he was flattered that she should write. And it was the novelty, the break in his routine, to which to his own surprise he found himself looking forward. So the invitation, which perhaps from a person better known would have caused no such reaction, became of importance. It was a peak in time to which he could anchor himself over the intervening days. A new person, a new relationship: who knew what might come of that?

Mrs Springer lived in Earl's Court. A disreputable, overcrowded area Mr Stone had always thought it, and he thought no better of it now. The entrance to the Underground station was filthy; in a street across the road a meeting of the British National Party was in progress, a man shouting himself hoarse from the back of a van. Behind neon lights and streaming glass windows the new-style coffee houses were packed; and the streets were full of young people in art-student dress and foreigners of every colour.

The address Mrs Springer gave turned out to be a private hotel in one of the crescents off the Earl's Court Road. A small typewritten 'Europeans Only' card below the bell proclaimed it a refuge of respectability and calm. It also turned out to be a refuge of age. A lift, as aged and tremulous as most of the people Mr Stone saw in the small lobby, took him up to Mrs Springer's room, where the bed was imperfectly disguised as a sofa, and the window, open because of the fug, framed a view of roofs and chimney pots against the murkily glowing sky. It was not what he expected, and the shabbiness was only partly redeemed by the presence of an elderly white-coated hotel servant whom Mrs Springer called Michael. Still, he passed a reasonable evening, was encouraged as before by Mrs Springer's brilliance, by the re-telling twice of the story of the cat and the cheese, to make a few witticisms of his own; though, as always now after brilliance, there came gloom.

He invited Mrs Springer to tea two Sundays afterwards, and made careful preparations to receive her. In these preparations Miss Millington, moving with what for her was sprightliness, showed an unwonted zeal. The fireplace was cleaned up, the cracked, uneven tiles polished to reveal their true discoloration, and a good fire got going. The cakes and scones were made ready, the table laid. Then, in the growing darkness, they waited.

When the bell rang they both went out to the draughty hall. The door was opened, Mrs Springer was revealed smiling crookedly, and Mr Stone, slightly confused, introduced Miss Millington.

'So this is the garden!' Mrs Springer said, lingering outside. With her shoe she touched a low leaf that was coated with pepper dust. At her touch the dust came off in flakes, and the leaf, somewhat wan, feebly reasserted its springiness.

'I suppose this is what is known as a shrub,' she said in her party way. 'What do you call it?'

'I don't really know,' Mr Stone said. 'It's been there for some years. It is a sort of evergreen, I imagine.'

'Miss Millington, what do the common people call this?'

In that moment Mr Stone lost Miss Millington.

'I don't know, mum,' Miss Millington said, 'what the proper name is. But the common people –'

But Mrs Springer had already moved on, having, even before entering the house, made herself mistress of it, as she had made herself mistress of both its occcupants.

In the second week of March Mr Stone and Mrs Springer were married, when on the tree in the school grounds the buds had swollen and in sunshine were like points of white.

2

Anxiety was replaced by a feeling of deflation, a certain fear and an extreme shyness, which became acute as the ritual bathroom hour approached on their first evening as man and wife, words which still mortified him. He waited, unwilling to mention the matter or to make the first move, and in the end it was she who went first. She was a long time and he, sucking on his burnt-out pipe, savoured the moments of privacy as something now to be denied him forever.

'Yours now, Richard.'

Her voice was no longer deep and actressy. It was attempting to tinkle, and emerged a blend of coo and halloo.

In the bathroom, which before had held his own smell, to him always a source of satisfaction, there was now a warm, scented dampness. Then he saw her teeth. It had never occurred to him that they might be false. He felt cheated and annoyed. Regret came to him, and a prick of the sharpest fear. Then he took out his own teeth and sadly climbed the steps to their bedroom.

He had never cared for the opinion of the street, refusing to bid anyone on it good-day for fear that such greeting might be imposed on him in perpetuity, leading to heaven knows what intimacy. But he did not want the street to suspect that his household had been modified, and it was his intention to have Margaret move in in instalments. He thought his plan had so far been successful. Two suitcases were almost enough for what Margaret had at the Earl's Court hotel, where their procession through the small dark lobby had attracted discreet stares from the old and frank, uncomprehending stares from the very old, making Mr Stone feel that he was engaged in an abduction, though Margaret's triumphant gravity suggested that the operation was one of rescue. They had arrived at their house in the early evening, as though for dinner; and Mr Stone had handled the suitcases with a certain careless authority to hint to whoever might be watching that the suitcases were his own.

They had scarcely settled down in bed, each silent in his own cot (Margaret in the one taken from the room where Olive occasionally slept), when she sat up, almost with her party brightness, and said, 'Richard, do you hear anything?'

Something he had heard. But now there was only silence. He settled down again, fearing speech from her.

Flap!

It was undeniable.

Thump! Creak! Measured noises, as of someone ascending the thinly-carpeted staircase firmly, cautiously.

'Richard, there is a man in the house!'

At her words the steps ceased.

'Go and look, Richard.'

He disliked the repetition of his name. But he dragged himself up to a sitting position. He thought she was relishing the role of the frightened woman, and he noted with distaste that she had pulled the blankets right up to her neck.

The responsibility was new. It wearied, irritated him. And though he was alarmed himself, he at that moment hoped that someone was in the house, standing right behind the door, and that he would come in and batter them both to death and release.

Flap, thump, flap.

He flung off the bedclothes and ran to the landing and put on the light, hoping by his speed and violence to still the noise, to drive it away.

'Hello!' he called. 'Who is it? Is there anyone there?'

There was no reply.

Carefully he approached the banister and looked down

the well of the stairs upon a gloom made sinister by the elongated leaning shadows of the rails. Far below him he saw the telephone, its dial dully gleaming.

He hurried back to the room. He closed the door, turned on the light. She was standing directly below the lampshade in her frilly nightdress, her mouth collapsed, her bed disarrayed, the inadequate sheet already peeling off the three large cushions (red, white and blue, and arranged by Miss Millington in that order) that served as mattress.

'I didn't see anyone,' he said with mild irritation, and sat down on his bed.

For some time they remained as they were, saying nothing. He looked about the room, avoiding her eye. He had always thought of his bedroom as comfortable. Now that it held a second person, he took it in detail by detail, and as he did so his irritation grew. The tasselled lampshade had been painted green by Miss Millington at his orders, not to cover grime but simply for the sake of the green; the lighted bulb now revealed the erratic distribution of all her labouring, overcharged brushstrokes. The curtains were made of three not quite matching pieces of brown velvet, chosen by Miss Millington to hide dirt. The carpet was worn, its design and colours no longer of importance; the cracked, ill-fitting linoleum surrounds (hard as metal) had lost their pattern and were a messy dark brown. The wallpaper was dingy, the ceiling cracked. Next to the dark, almost black wardrobe a ruined armchair, which had not been sat on for years, served as a receptacle for miscellaneous objects.

Flap! Creak! Thump!

'Richard! Dial 999, Richard!'

He realized the necessity, but was greatly afraid.

'Come down with me to the telephone,' he said.

He would willingly have had her precede him down the steps, but his new responsibility did not permit this. Arming himself with a bent poker, dusty to the touch, he tiptoed down the stairs ahead of her, expecting a blow from every dark corner of his once familiar house. Arriving at the hall, he telephoned, poker in hand, regretting his action as soon as he heard the cool, unhurried inquiries.

They went upstairs to wait, turning on all lights on the way and recoving their teeth from the bathroom. Except for their own movements there was now silence.

When the bell rang Mr Stone went down to the door with the poker in his hand. The officer, armed only with an electric torch, gave the poker an amused look, and Mr Stone began to apologize for it.

The officer cut him short. 'I've sent my man round to the back,' he said, and proceeded, expertly and reassuringly, to dive into all the corners that had held such threat.

They found no one.

The constable who had been sent round to the back came in through the front door; and they all sat in the still warm sitting-room.

'With some of these semi-detached houses noises next door often sound as though they're coming from this side,' the officer said.

The constable smiled, playing with his torch.

'There was a man in the house,' Margaret said argumentatively.

'Is there any door or entrance in the back he could get in by?' the officer asked.

'I don't know,' she said. 'I only came to the house tonight.'

There was a silence. Mr Stone looked away.

'Would you like a cup of tea?' he asked. From the films he had seen he believed that police officers always drank tea in such circumstances.

'Yes,' Margaret said, 'do have a cup of tea.'

The tea was declined, their apologies politely brushed aside.

But the house blazed with lights, and the police car attracted attention. So that on the following day, far from attempting to hide his marriage, Mr Stone was compelled to proclaim it and to endure the furtive glances, the raised curtains of the street.

Even Miss Millington, used to curious happenings in the house during her absence, could not hide her excitement at the police visit.

One thing relieved him. They had come to one another as wits. And when, towards the end of their pre-marriage acquaintance (the word 'courtship' did not appeal to him), his efforts grew febrile, he had sought to establish himself as someone with a rich sense of humour and an eye for the ridiculous in 'life'. He feared, then, that marriage might mean a lifelong and exhausting violation of his personality. But to his surprise he found that Margaret required no high spirits from him, no jocularity, no wit; and again to his surprise he discovered that her party manner, which he had thought part of her personality, was something she discarded almost at once, reserving it for those of her friends who knew her reputation. And often during their after-dinner silence (he reading the paper, Margaret writing letters or knitting, thin-rimmed spectacles low down her nose, ageing her considerably) he would think with embarrassment for both their sakes of the brightness of her first remark to him, its needle-sharp enunciation ('Do you . . . like *cats*?'), and of the unexpected brilliance of his last remark at that meeting ('I imagine that's why they're called nuts'). For never again was she so impressively abrupt or 'brittle' (a word whose meaning he thought he fully understood only after meeting Margaret), and never again was he so brilliant.

Of Margaret's history he never inquired, and she volunteered little. The thought sometimes arose, though he suppressed it, for Margaret by her behaviour had signalled that what they had said during their 'courtship' was to be discounted, that she was not as grand as she had made out. Neither was he; and this was more painful. For his own secrets, which had never been secrets until the night of their meeting, had to be revealed. His head librarianship, for example, and his £1,000 a year. Margaret asked no questions. But secrets were burdensome; he lacked the patience or the energy to conceal or deceive. Neither his position nor salary was negligible, but he felt that Margaret had expected more and that secretly she mocked at him, as he secretly mocked at her, though his own mockery he considered harmless.

Secretly she might mock, but of this nothing escaped her in speech or expression. And it was astonishing to what degree he was able to recreate his former routine. He was out all day at the office as before; and Margaret at home became an extension, a more pervading extension, of Miss Millington, who had accepted the new situation and her new mistress with greater calm than her master. Certain things he lost. His solitude was one; never again would he return to an empty house. And there was the relationship with Olive. Though she was all goodwill and though he might try to pretend that their relationship remained what it was, he knew that a further falsity, more corroding than that introduced by the birth of Gwen, had invaded it. And then there was the smell, the feel of his house.

The mustiness, the result of ineffectual fussings with broom and brush by Miss Millington, in which he had taken so much pleasure, was replaced not by the smell of polish and soap but by a new and alien mustiness. The sitting-room for some weeks he could scarcely call his own, for it was dominated by a tigerskin, which came out of store in excellent condition and which Margaret explained by producing a framed sepia photograph of a dead tiger on whose chest lay the highly polished boot of an English cavalry officer, moustached, sitting bolt upright in a heavy wooden armchair (brought from goodness knows where), fighting back a smile, one hand caressing a rifle laid neatly across his thighs, with three sorrowful, top-heavily turbanned Indians, beaters or bearers or whatever they were, behind him. Many little bits of furniture came with the tigerskin as well. Very fussy frilly bits he thought them, and they looked out of place among the bulky nineteen-thirty furniture which was his own. But Miss Millington, falling on them with a delight as of one rediscovering glories thought dead and gone, regularly and indefatigably heightened their gloss, using a liquid polish which, drying in difficult crevices, left broken patterns of pure, dusty white. To accommodate the new furniture there had to be rearrangements. Miss Millington and Margaret consulted and rearranged, Miss Millington with painful joy, eyes closed, lips compressed, wisps of grey wet hair escaping from her hair net, doing the pushing and hauling about. So afternoon after afternoon Mr Stone returned home to a disturbing surprise, and the expectant glances of the two women waiting approval.

Before his marriage he had been to Miss Millington an employer. Now he became The Master. And to the two women he was something more. He was a 'man', a creature of particular tastes, aptitudes and authority. It was as a man that he left the house every morning – or rather, was sent off, spick and span and spruce and correct in every way, as though the world was now his audience – and it was as a man that he returned. This aspect of his new responsibility deepened his feeling of inadequacy; he even felt a little fraudulent. Miss Millington, in particular, appeared confidently to await a change in his attitude and behaviour towards her, and he felt that he was continually letting her down. He had been a 'man' in a limited way and only for a few days at a time with his sister Olive; it was an intermittent solace which he welcomed but which he was at the end always glad to escape. Now there was no escape.

From his role as their brave bull, going forth day after day to 'business' (Miss Menzies's word, which was Margaret's as well), he hoped to find rest in the office. But rest there was none, for increasingly his manner, to his disquiet, reflected his role. The neatness on which he prided himself became a dapperness. And even if one forgot the irreverent allusions of the young to his married state, in the beginning a source of much pain to him, there was a noticeable change in the attitude of the office people. The young girls no longer petted him or flirted with him, and he could not imagine himself making as if to hit them on the bottom with his cylindrical ruler, the weapon with which he repelled their playful advances. And as he progressively lost his air of freedom and acquired the appearance of one paroled from a woman's possession, the young men, even those who were married, no longer tolerated him as before, no longer pretended that he might be one of them. He attracted instead the fatiguing attentions of Wilkinson, the office Buddhist, whose further eccentricity was sometimes to walk about the office corridors in stockinged feet.

He had fallen into the habit of staying in the office later than was usual or necessary, as though to recapture a little of the privacy and solitude he had lost. Turning off the library lights one evening, and going into the darkened corridor, he bumped into a man as tall as himself. The man's clothes felt rough; he was a guardsman. And a girl's voice (he recognized one of the typists) said a little breathlessly, 'We can't find the light switch, Mr Stone.' He showed where it was. He did more: he turned the lights on. And it was only when he was on the train, his briefcase containing the evening papers resting lightly on his lap, that he realized the truth of the situation. 'Damned fool,' he thought, his anger directed as much towards himself as towards them. He took a dislike to that typist and was glad when not long afterwards she left the office.

The office not offering refuge, he was driven to seek it at home, so that his goings forth and returnings were both in the nature of flights, until at length he found that he had settled down into the new life, had grown to expect that as soon as he opened the garden gate the front door should be opened by a sprucer Miss Millington, that Margaret, who had given the signal for the opening, should be in the front window and should from that point advance, at first as though to receive him, and then to embrace him, brushing off some of the fresh powder from her cheeks on to his. She dressed every afternoon for his return as carefully as she dressed him for his departure in the mornings.

The street still watched, especially for this evening encounter. And, as an aid to composure, it became his custom to start whistling as soon as he came within sight of the house. 'That was very nice, Richard,' Margaret said one day as she kissed him. 'This doggie is for sale.' He had been whistling, 'How Much is That Doggie in the Window?' So he whistled it every evening. And that was how he became 'Doggie' and, more rarely, she became 'Doggie'.

Yet, communing with his tree, he could not help contrasting its serenity with his disturbance. It would shed its leaves in time; but this would lead to a renewal which would bring greater strength. Responsibility had come too late to him. He had broken the pattern of his life, and this break could at best be only healed. It would not lead to renewal. So the tree no longer comforted. It reproached.

This summer the Male was busier than ever, building an outhouse. More fervently than before, Mr Stone wished for some accident that would put an end to the man's never-ending improvements to his nest, which improvements were watched with unabating admiration by the man's numerous brood.

He was a man, then. Bravely every morning he ventured forth into the rigorous world of business. And now he learned that Margaret was a woman. She attached the greatest importance to her functions as a woman and a wife. These were to feed, dress, humour, encourage, occasionally to seduce and never to let down. She rested in the mornings to recover from her exertions in seeing him off; she rested in the afternoons before getting ready for his return; she was concerned about getting her sleep at night so that she did not look a fright in the morning. Many creams and skin-foods supplemented her rest. And he was not grateful. He refused to notice. He began to think her idle, lazy, vain. When he thought of the responsibility she had imposed on him, when he thought of her pulling the blankets up to her neck on their first night, he could not help feeling that in the division of their functions she had got the better bargain.

The emphasis on the separateness of their functions as man and woman was a standing irritation. He would have liked her to relieve him of the garden, but she was unwilling to do so. Not only because she didn't care for gardening –

the pre-marriage statement turned out to have a grain of truth – but also because she thought it suitable that a man should have a hobby and that gardening should be the hobby of Mr Stone, who had no other aptitude. Twice a day (thrice on Sundays) he faced her across the dining table; and these moments, which in no consideration of marriage he had envisaged, were moments of the greatest strain. She, the feeder, ate with voracious appetite, continually apologizing for being slow. He could see the powder on the hairs of her taut cheeks. Her lipstick became oily; then, as it grew fainter, spread over areas not originally painted. Reflecting at the dining table on her idleness and frivolity, the hours she spent preparing herself for him, he feared he might say something offensive. But their first quarrel occurred for another, ridiculous reason.

At Margaret's suggestion, and against his wishes, they gave a dinner party, which to a large extent recreated one of the Tomlinsons' dinner parties. It was, inevitably, somewhat shabbier, even Margaret's improving zeal having failed to make any great impression on the house which had been so carefully neglected for so long. The Tomlinsons themselves came, radiating patronage and benevolence, their manner suggesting that they regarded themselves as creators of the new establishment. There were various friends of Margaret's, some picked up from the Tomlinsons', one or two from the Earl's Court hotel. (How little he knew of her!) Among the friends was a tall, heavy woman of forty or fifty with a face scrubbed of all attraction and expression; she didn't speak, little attention was paid to her, and yet, sitting primly where she was put, she appeared content.

Mr Stone had been urged to get some of his business colleagues. But he could think of no one. Evans, Keenan, Wilkinson, none of them was really suitable. Evans might have done, but he would have accepted, if he had accepted, as one doing a favour. With his colleagues Mr Stone had only an office relationship, of the utmost cordiality, but over the years of his bachelorhood the relationship had hardened in this way, so that any visiting now would have appeared an intrusion; such visiting in any case seemed more in evidence among the young. Nor did Mr Stone relish meeting his colleagues outside the office. After the initial boisterous greeting, which suggested that there was so much in common, so much to say, after the cracking of the current office joke, conversation faded, having little to feed on, until one of them said with brisk joviality, 'Well, see you at the office.' It was only at the office that such relationships could flourish; they were like hothouse plants, needing the protection of their artificial setting.

From Mr Stone's side, then, the only persons who came were Olive and Gwen. He was outnumbered. He couldn't count Miss Millington as one of his allies. She, donning hair net and scarf, and panting and sighing and breaking into cold sweat, had zestfully worked all day long under Margaret's directions. And then, to her own gasping delight, she had been dressed for the dinner by Margaret in a new apron and new cap which, tilting sharply back from her low brow, had given a touch of rakishness to her aged baby-face. Nor could Mr Stone count Gwen on his side. Pallid and pimply and sour, the fat creature sought to convey her impatient contempt for everyone. She deeply disturbed Mr Stone, already vulnerable in his new role as husband and host.

With the wine – 'I think a good Beaujolais would do,' Margaret had said, trespassing on the role of her husband after he had shown no wish to take it on – there were toasts. Not many, for only one bottle of Beaujolais had been bought and this was poured out like a liqueur, one small glass per guest, as was the custom at the Tomlinsons'. Then, as was also customary at the Tomlinsons', the men and women separated. With all the delight of a fulfilled woman in the segregation of the sexes, Margaret shooed the women away from the dining-room, leaving Mr Stone, Tomlinson and one other man (the party was unbalanced, many of the women being widows) in silence, Mr Stone not knowing what to say, Tomlinson looking anguished, clearing his throat, the other man (an accountant, a chief accountant) beginning to speak but only a squeak issuing from a throat clogged after a long silence.

'Very good dinner you gave us,' Tomlinson said at last, in encouraging commendation.

'Yes,' the chief accountant said hurriedly. 'Very good.'

They listened to the shuffle and contented babble of the women. Margaret's voice was deep, Grace drawled. There was nothing to drink in the dining-room (there was none at the Tomlinsons'). Once, several Christmas-week dinners ago, Tomlinson had attempted to tell a dirty story. Everyone had dutifully prepared to listen, smile and perhaps even make laughter that would be heard outside the room. But Tomlinson had told his story so precisely, with such calculated pauses and smiles, yet with such evident distaste on his thin, tormented face, that the story had fallen flat, no one knowing when it had ended, no one laughing, everyone embarrassed and slightly shocked, for without wit the story had appeared only as a piece of wilful obscenity. Tomlinson had thereafter abandoned his role of male-amuser. So now they stood, waiting.

'I think we can go outside now,' Mr Stone said. He was unwilling to use the phrase about joining the ladies; he did not feel he could manage it with Tomlinson's ease and conviction.

'Not yet,' Tomlinson said, as though his authority had been appealed to.

And indeed at that moment came the sound of the lavatory flush.

The chief accountant cleared his throat.

When at last they did go outside, Margaret greeted them with, 'Well, what have you men been guffawing about?'

They seated themselves around the tigerskin like participants in some form of combat. Mr Stone submitted with outward good humour and inward fury to the badinage about his marriage, though he could not help contracting his brows in annoyance when Grace Tomlinson said, 'I see you've already trained him well, Margaret.'

The entertainment was like that at the Tomlinsons'.

There was singing. And, as at the Tomlinsons', the women were expected to sing well and to be applauded seriously. Occasionally, very occasionally, there might be an acknowleged comedienne. But the men were supposed to clown, savage creatures who, presenting forbidding fronts to the world of business, relaxed thus in the privacy of their hearths for their mates and friends alone, revealing benignant or childish aspects of their character which the outside world never suspected. So he did ridiculous things to the lapels of his jacket, pulled his hair down his forehead, rolled up one trouser leg, and with the two other sad men did his comic song.

It was after this that Margaret asked Gwen to recite 'something nice'. To Mr Stone's surprise Gwen rose at once, the back of her flared skirt crumpled from the clumsy weight so recently on it, and took up her position on the tigerskin. She did a scene from *The Importance of Being Earnest*, affecting a deep voice not for the male role but, in imitation of the celebrated actress, for the female. Mr Stone looked on in wonder; up till that moment he had not thought Gwen capable of doing anything. Her sour expression had been replaced by one of blankness, as though she had removed herself from the room. With complete absorption she acted out the scene, turning her head abruptly this way and that to indicate the changing of roles. She never faltered or lost her composure, even when, attempting an excessive throatiness for *In a Handbag*, she emitted *hand* as a squeak. There was a good deal of approval, which Mr Stone shared.

It then occurred to him that it was perhaps indelicate of Gwen to imitate the actress whom Margaret imitated, in a circle which had for so long accepted Margaret's imitation. He glanced at Margaret and saw that she was suffering slightly. The line that ran from nose to mouth had deepened; her lips had tautened over her false teeth. He was filled with sympathy for her. But when the performance came to an end it was Margaret who led the applause, crying 'Bravo! Bravo!'

With a well-trained bow Gwen acknowledged the applause, not seeming, however, to see anyone in the room.

And then to the general surprise she launched into a fresh recitation, the court scene from *The Merchant of Venice*. This was less successful. Whereas before she had spoken prose as though it were rhetoric, now she spoke rhetoric as though it were everyday speech. Mr Stone could hardly recognise Portia's speech. Then, turning her head to indicate the new speaker, Gwen attempted Shylock, and attempted Shylock in a Jewish accent.

Something told Mr Stone this was wrong and, looking about the room, he saw proof on every face. Grace Tomlinson, whose lips were invariably slightly parted, now had her mouth clamped shut. Tomlinson looked stern. Margaret's eyes held definite anger. Everyone shot brief covert glances at the chief accountant, whose eyes were fixed on Gwen.

The recitation went on, only Olive in her pride unaware of the currents of disapproval and embarrassment.

The recitation was over. Without waiting for applause, Gwen bowed and returned to her seat, smoothing her dress below her and then looking down at her lap like one annoyed, like one whose modesty had been violated, while shufflings and rustlings broke through the room.

'Miss Banks,' Margaret said coldly, 'did you bring your music?'

The person addressed was the tall woman with the scrubbed face. Little attention had been paid to her, but she had remained all evening in her own pool of contentment. At the dining table she had shown herself a silent and steady eater. Now, without replying, she took out her music from her very large bag, rose, seated herself at the piano and began to play.

In the stillness that followed – Miss Banks's music received exaggerated attention – Mr Stone had much time for thought. He thought about Miss Banks and he thought about his house. What changes had come to it! The neighbours could now hear piano music. Yet from the outside his house had not changed at all. What strange things must happen behind the blank front doors of so many houses! And just as sometimes when travelling on a train he had mentally stripped himself of train, seats and passengers and seen himself moving four or five feet above ground in a sitting posture at forty miles an hour, so now he was assailed by a vision of the city stripped of stone and concrete and timber and metal, stripped of all buildings, with people suspended next to and above and below one another, going through all the motions of human existence. And he had a realization, too upsetting to be more than momentarily examined, that all that was solid and immutable and enduring about the world, all to which man linked himself (The Monster watering her spring flowers, The Male expanding his nest), flattered only to deceive. For all that was not flesh was irrelevant to man, and all that was important was man's own flesh, his weakness and corruptibility.

The dinner party had its ridiculous sequel two weeks later. Every four weeks or so Olive sent Mr Stone a fruit cake of her own making. The custom had survived Olive's marriage, had survived Gwen. Mr Stone was glad that it had survived his own marriage as well and that Margaret, however much she might dislike this reminder of an additional claim on her husband's manhood, had lent herself happily to the ritual of cutting Olive's cake.

But this evening when, the cake cut, the coffee ready, they sat before the electric fire, Margaret did a strange thing. She speared a large piece of the cake with her knife and held it close to the guard of the fire.

'You will electrocute yourself!' Mr Stone cried.

The rich cake had already caught. Margaret jerked it off on to the reflector. It burned steadily and well, like good fuel. Even when completely charred it continued to burn, the metal around it turning brown from the oozing fat.

'In India,' Margaret said, gazing at the cake, 'they always offer little bits like this to the fire before they cook or eat anything.'

Mr Stone was outraged. Starting to put down his plate gently, as he always did, but changing his mind right at the last moment and setting it down hard, he got up and made for the door, kicking at the tiger's head, against which he had nearly tripped.

'Doggie!'

He held the door open. 'I – I don't believe you've ever been to India.'

'Doggie!'

He locked himself in the former junk room, which Margaret had furnished with some of her furniture and presented to him as a 'study', a place for male solitude. And there, despite Margaret's knocks and calls and coos, he remained, thinking in the dark of the past, of Olive, himself, childhood. He beheld a boy of seventeen walking back alone from school on a winter's day, past the shops of the High Street. The boy was going home, unaware of what awaited him there. Whether the picture was true or composite he no longer knew; whether there was a reason for remembering this stretch of the way home he couldn't say. But it was what he saw when he wished to think of his childhood in a tender way. This boy didn't know that his life would unroll without disturbance, the years flow evenly; and for him Mr Stone felt an ache of pity.

At length the passion passed. It was quite late and he was stiff and cold. He nevertheless prolonged his stay in the study until past ten. Then, for no reason, he went down to the sitting-room. Margaret did not speak; she was reading a library book. He said nothing to her. He went up to the bathroom. It had become the rule that he should go first. It was also a rule that he should smoke his pipe there; it warmed the room up, Margaret said, and she loved the smell of his tobacco. It was his custom therefore to puff vigorously on his pipe four or five times before leaving the bathroom. Tonight, because of their quarrel, he went without his pipe.

From the bedroom he listened to her own preparations. When she came in he was under the sheets, motionless. She did not put the light on. She set the alarm and got into bed.

He was falling off to sleep when he heard her.

'Doggie.'

He didn't reply.

Minutes later she spoke again.

'Doggie.'

He mumbled.

'Doggie, you've made me very unhappy.'

Whereat he almost lost his temper. Fatigue alone kept him silent.

She started to sob.

'Doggie, I want to eat a piece of your cake.'

'Why don't you go and eat the damned thing?'

She sobbed a little more.

'Won't you come and eat a little piece with me, Doggie?'

'No.'

'A little piece, Doggie.'

'For heaven's sake!' he said, throwing the bedclothes off.

She was sitting up.

They went to the bathroom and got their teeth. They went down to the sitting-room, almost stuffy after the cold bedroom, and ate large pieces of Olive's cake in silence.

Then they went up to the bathroom and took out their teeth, and went to bed, still silent.

He was now wide awake.

'Doggie,' she said.

'Doggie.'

It was some time before they could fall asleep, and they suffered frightfully from indigestion.

Olive continued to send her cakes. But Mr Stone knew that the relationship between his sister and himself belonged to the past.

So step by step he became married; and step by step marriage grew on him. For Margaret revealed a plasticity of character which abridged and rendered painless the process of getting to know her, getting used to her. He was at the core of their relationship; she moulded herself about him so completely and comfortingly that it was with surprise, when he observed her with her friends, that he remembered she did have a character of her own, and views and attitudes. And just as at first it seemed that Margaret had become an extension of Miss Millington, so he now saw them both as extensions of himself. It was, too, with a growing pleasure, which he did not in the beginning care to acknowledge even to himself, that he thought of the suspension that came to the house as soon as he left it in the morning, and of its reanimation in the afternoon in preparation to receive him.

His habits were converted into rituals; they grew sacred even to him. He succumbed to gardening, of the type that Margaret desired, his attentions to beds and bulbs being regarded as sacramental by both Margaret and Miss Millington, willing acolytes (Miss Millington, whose only concern with the garden before had been to dust it, in her uncontrolled, deluging and expensive way, with pepper dust, and perhaps, when flowers appeared, to make some reference to their loveliness). So it was established that he was 'fond of gardening'. But he drew the line when Margaret, saying, 'Something for you, Doggie,' tried to get him to become a regular listener to *Country Questions* and *In Your Garden.* He soothed her disappointment by repeating, what he had heard in the office, that the people who spoke on the radio with rustic accents about country matters lived in Mayfair; window-boxes were the only land *they* knew. This became one of his 'sayings'; his statements had never before been regarded as 'sayings'.

It was established, too, that the black cat next door was an enemy. The two women entered into a sweet conspiracy to conceal the creature's activities from the Master. An intermittent afternoon watch was kept, and ravages hastily repaired so that the Master might not be upset when he returned. The women succeeded better than they knew. The war taken out of his hands, Mr Stone's hostility towards the cat diminished, leaving him with a sense of something lost.

But beneath the apparent calm which marriage had once more brought to him, there grew a new appreciation of time. It was flying by. It was eating up his life. Every week –

and how quickly these Sundays followed one another on the radio: *Coast and Country* after the news, or *The Countryside in October, The Countryside in November*, monthly programmes that seemed like weekly programmes: Sundays which made him feel that the last one was yesterday – every racing week drew him nearer to retirement, inactivity, corruption. Every ordered week reminded him of failure, of the uncreative years once so comfortingly stacked away in his mind. Every officeless Sunday sharpened his anxiety, making him long for Monday and the transient balm of the weekdays, false though he knew their fullness to be, in spite of the office diary he had begun to keep, tabulating appointments, things to be done, to flatter himself that he was busily and importantly occupied.

The tree, changing, developing with the year, made its point every day. And when, sitting at the Sunday tea, trying to reassure himself by his precise, neat, slow gestures, he sometimes said, 'You are part of me, Margaret. I don't know what I would do without you,' he spoke with an urgency and gratitude she did not fully understand.

3

Late in March, the buds white in sunlight on the black branches and daily acquiring a greenish tinge, Mr Stone and Margaret left London for a fortnight. It was his holiday – he who would soon be in need of no holiday – and it was also their honeymoon. They went to Cornwall. Mr Stone preferred to spend his holidays in England. He had thought after the war that he would go abroad. In 1948 he went to Ireland; but the most enjoyable part of that holiday was the journey from Southampton to Cobh in a luxurious, rationing-free American liner. A fortnight in Paris two years later had been, after the first moment of pleasure at being in the celebrated city, a tedious torment. He had dutifully gone sightseeing and had been considerably fatigued; he often wondered afterwards why he followed the guidebook so slavishly and went to places as dreary as the Panthéon and the Invalides. He had sat in the cafés, but hated the coffee, and to sit idling in an unfamiliar place was not pleasant, and the cups of coffee were so small. He had tried aperitifs but had decided they were a waste of time and money. He was very lonely; his pocket was playfully picked by an Algerian, who warned him to be more careful in future; everything was hideously expensive; the incessant cries from men and women of *le service, monsieur, le service!* had given him a new view of the French, whom he had thought a frivolous, fun-loving people made a little sad by the war. And for the last two days he was afflicted by a type of dysentery which made it impossible for him to take anything more solid than mineral water.

So Cornwall it was. Margaret suppressed her disappointment in reflections about the need to economize, which, already delicately acknowledged, had begun to obtrude more and more into their conversation, now that Mr Stone was only eighteen months or so from retirement. She told Grace Tomlinson, and Grace agreed, that it was high time they got to know their own country.

They put up at the Queen's Hotel in Penzance. The season had not properly begun. The weather was unusually bad, the hotel people said, as though assuring them they had not done a foolish thing; and they received much attention.

They took buses and went for walks, Mr Stone feeling conspicuous in his black city overcoat (Simpson's, and twenty years old: Simpson's clothes, as he and Tomlinson had long ago agreed, were worth the extra money, and it had once been a source of satisfaction to Mr Stone that he was often, so far as dress went, a complete Simpson's man). In another part of England he might have felt less conspicuous in his black overcoat. But in that landscape it was like an emblem of softness and inaptitude. Human habitation had scarcely modified the land; it was not as if a race had withdrawn but as if, growing less fit, it had been expunged from the stone-bound land, which remained to speak of discord between man and earth.

Once on a bare cliff they came upon a dead fox, as whole as the living animal, no marks of death or violence on it, lying on its side as if in sleep, its fur blown about by the wind.

On Sunday they went to Chysauster. It was a difficult walk, and for part of the way led down a murderous rocky lane. The wind was sharp and naggingly irregular, the sunshine thin and fitful. By the time they arrived they were both bad-tempered, in no mood for abandoned Celtic dwellings. They sat against a low stone wall in the lee of the wind, Mr Stone reckless of his overcoat, and worked through the tea they had brought, the carrying of which had added to their discomfort. From time to time, but never long enough to warm them, the sun came out.

Afterwards, like giants entering the houses of men, they examined the cluster of solid stone hovels. How thick the walls, how clumsy, how little space they enclosed, as though built for people sheltering from more than the elements! Mr Stone thought of the Monster with her watering can, the nest-building of the Male: this was not their setting. Then he remembered his own Simpson's coat. He saw himself, a cartoon figure, with knotted club and leopard skin: he could not hold the picture for long. The hovels were indefinably depressing. He wanted to get away.

They had planned to get a bus to St Ives and from there to get another back to Penzance. In the hotel room, with maps and bus time-tables, such an adventurous return had seemed simple enough. But the walk to Chysauster had taken longer than they expected; and now they could not determine where they were. Margaret, proclaiming her stupidity in these matters, left the fixing of their position to him, and with wind and cheating sun his temper was wearing thin again.

Then they saw the fire. Across the dry bare field at the back of the hut-cluster it advanced silently towards them with much clean white smoke.

And they saw they were not alone. To their left, considering the fire and not them, was a very tall, big-boned man in a dark-blue beret and a tattered, unbuttoned army tunic. He looked like a farm labourer. His elongated heavy face was dark red; his eyes were small, the lips puffed and raw.

Mr Stone felt urgently now that they should be off.

'How do we get to the road for St Ives?' he asked, and found himself shouting, as though his words would otherwise be overcome by the smoke of the silent fire.

The man in the army tunic didn't speak. He glanced at them, then started walking briskly away with long-legged strides. Over the wall that separated the huts from the field he went, and along a white path in the field itself, walking into the smoke.

And hurriedly, not willing to lose sight of him, they followed, scrambling over the wall.

The man was disappearing into the smoke.

Mr Stone knew panic.

The man stopped, turned towards them, and was lost in smoke. And they followed.

They heard the low, contented crackle of the fire. Smoke enveloped them. They were robbed of earth and reality. He was robbed of judgement, of the will to act.

Then Margaret's cry, 'Doggie!' recalled him to questioning and fear, and they ran back to the wall, out of the smoke, into the clear open air, to rocks and earth and sky.

Behind the wall they stood, watching the fire. It came right up to the wall and before their eyes burnt itself out. The smoke was dissipated in the air. And it was as if there had been no fire, and all that had happened a hallucination.

Reality was completed by the arrival of a Morris Minor. Mr Stone inquired about the road to St Ives. The new visitors offered a lift to Penzance.

It was only when they were in the car that they saw, not far from the stone huts, the man in the army tunic. He was gazing at the only slightly charred field. He did not look at them.

'Well, of course,' the desk-clerk said confidingly, when Margaret gave him an account of the afternoon's happenings, 'the thing about Cornwall' – his Birmingham accent prolonging the *g* like a piano pedal – 'is that it is steeped in legend. Positively steeped.'

Mr Stone never doubted that the incident could be rationally and simply explained. But that hallucinatory moment, when earth and life and senses had been suspended, remained with him. It was like an experience of nothingness, an experience of death.

They decided to give the Cornwall of legend the miss – the desk-clerk told with relish of a man he knew whose house had been burned down after a visit to Chysauster – and they were helped by the weather, which continued cold, drizzly and uncertain. The day before they left, however, the skies cleared and in the afternoon they went for a walk. Their way led along cliffs which, rimmed with deep white footpaths, fell to the sea in partial ruin, on a principle of destruction that was easy to comprehend but was on such a scale that the mind could not truly grasp it. It was still cold, and they encountered no more than half a dozen people on the way, among them a man who, to Mr Stone's satisfaction, was wearing a black city overcoat. Just when they were getting tired and craving for sweet things, they saw a neat sign promising tea fifty yards on.

The establishment was as neat as the sign. A clean white card on each crisp checked tablecloth, a blue cloth alternating with a red, announced the owner as Miss Chichester. Miss Chichester was what her name, her establishment and her card promised. She was middle-aged, stout, with a large bosom. Her brisk manner proclaimed the dignity of labour as a discovery she expected to be universally shared; her accent was genteel without exaggeration; in her dress and discreet make-up there was the hint, that though perhaps widowed and in straitened circumstances, she was not letting herself go.

Only one of the tables was occupied, by a party of three, a man and two women. The women were as stout as Miss Chichester, but an overflow of flesh here and there, a coarseness in legs, complexion and hair, in coats, hats and shiny new bags suggested only a cosy grossness, as well as the fixed stares through spectacles in ill-chosen frames, and the smooth swollen hands firmly grasping bags on thighs whose fatness was accentuated by the opened coats, lower buttons alone undone. The man was a wizened creature with narrow, sloping shoulders loose within a stiff new tweed jacket, his thin hair, the flex of his hearing-aid and the steel rims of his spectacles contributing to a general impression of perilous attenuation, as did the hand-rolled cigarette which, thin and wrinkled like the neck of the smoker, lay dead and forgotten between thin lips. He showed no interest in the arrival of Margaret and Mr Stone, and continued to stare at the checked tablecloth, sitting between the two women (one his wife, the other – what?) who looked like his keepers.

Their silence imposed silence on Margaret and Mr Stone as well, and even when Miss Chichester brought out tea for the party the silence continued. The man fell wordlessly on plates and pots and tasteful jugs as though he had been sparing his energies for this moment. He attacked the dainty sandwiches, the fresh scones, the home-made jam; and with every mouthful he appeared to grow more energetic, restless and enterprising. His thin, hairy hand shot out in all directions, making to grab teapots, cake-plates, jam-bowls, gestures so decisive and of such authority that his keepers, who were at first inclined to deflect his pouncing actions, surrendered entirely, and contented themselves with salvaging what food they could. Abruptly the eater finished. He worked his lips over his teeth, made a few sucking noises, and perceptibly the expression of blind eagerness gave way to the earlier sour dejection. He stared straight ahead, at nothing; while his keepers, rescuing their tea interlude from premature extinction, intermittently nibbled at bread and butter as if without appetite. Throughout there had been no speech at the table.

The habit of examining people older than himself was one into which Mr Stone had been falling during the past year. It was something he fought against; observation told him that only women, very young children and very old men inspected and assessed others of their group with such intensity. But now in spite of himself he stared with horror and fascination, and found that, as the eater's actions had grown more frenzied, his own had grown exaggeratedly slow.

Their own tea arrived and they prepared to begin. Attempting to break the silence Mr Stone found that he whispered, and the whisper was like gunshot. Silence continued, except for the kitchen clatter and the thumps of Miss Chichester's shoes.

And then silence vanished. The door was pushed vigorously open and there entered a very tall fair man and a very small fair girl. The man was in mountaineering clothes, like one equipped for a Himalayan or at least Alpine expedition. He carried rucksack and ropes; his thick rough trousers were tucked into thick woollen socks, and these disappeared into massive lustreless boots with extraordinarily thick soles. He created, by his masculine entry and the laying down of detachable burdens, as much noise as for two or three. The girl was soft and mute. Her slacks, imperfectly and tremulously filled, suggested only fragility; so did her light-blue silk scarf. The pale colours of her clothes, the milky fawn of her raincoat, and the style of her pale tan shoes marked her as a European.

Sitting at the table, his rough-trousered knees reaching to the tablecloth, dwarfing the table and the flower vase, the mountaineer extended a greeting, accompanied by a bow, to the room. His English was only slightly accented.

The eater and his keepers nodded. Mr Stone's eyebrows dropped, like one surprised and affronted. Margaret was only momentarily distracted from scones and jam.

But the man filled the room. His speech created a conversational momentum on its own; the silence of others did not matter. He said that he was Dutch; that in his country there were no mountains; that Cornwall was indescribably picturesque. All this in English which, because he was Dutch, was perfect; and the linguistic performance was made more impressive by his occasional sentences in Dutch to his mute scarfed companion.

He required no replies, but the eater and his keepers were steadily drawn into his talk. From nods and exclamations of 'Yes' and 'Oh!' they went on to speak approvingly of his English. These remarks the Dutchman translated to his companion, who, raising embarrassed eyes, appeared to receive the compliments as her own.

'S-so –' the eater began, and rolled his wrinkled cigarette between his lips. 'S-so you're on holiday?' His voice was thin and curiously querulous.

'A fortnight's holiday,' the Dutchman said.

The eater chewed at his cigarette. 'I – I retired last Friday.'

The Dutchman spoke to his companion in Dutch.

'Forty years with the same firm,' the eater said joylessly.

His keepers glanced at Margaret and Mr Stone, inviting them to take cognition of the information just given.

'Forty years,' Margaret said, swallowing cake. 'That's very nice.'

'Very nice indeed,' said the Dutchman.

And now the keepers had broad smiles for everyone. 'Show them, Fred,' one said.

'On Friday,' Fred said, his face as sourly dejected as before, his voice as querulous, 'I had a party. They gave it for me.' He was having difficulty with his words and his throat. He paused, swallowed and added, 'In my honour.' His hand went to his vest pocket. 'They gave me this.'

A keeper passed the watch to the Dutchman.

'Forty years,' Fred said.

'Very nice,' said the Dutchman, and spoke in Dutch.

His companion looked up, reddening, and smiled at Fred.

The keeper, recovering the watch, passed it to Margaret.

'Now isn't ... that ... *nice*?' Margaret said, looking from the watch to Fred and speaking as to a child who must be encouraged. 'Isn't this nice, Richard?'

'Very nice.'

'They gave it to me on Friday,' Fred said. 'Retired on Friday –'

'Brought him down here on Saturday,' the head keeper said triumphantly.

Now Fred was really unwinding. 'Read the inscription,' he said, handing the watch back to Mr Stone. 'It's on the back. It was a sort of surprise, you know. Of course there was a lot of whispering –'

'Very nice,' Mr Stone said, holding out the watch.

'Show it to her,' Fred commanded, indicating Margaret. 'But what's so funny about a last day, I said. Last day's same as any other. Last day's just another –'

'Very nice,' Margaret said.

'May I?' the Dutchman said, reaching out.

'I wasn't looking for medals. That's all that a lot of these young fellows are doing these days. Looking for medals. Young fellow comes up to me and asks for the keys. I say, "You take them, mate. *I* ain't looking for no medals."'

Noticing his moodiness on the way back, Margaret said, 'Don't worry, Doggie. I'll buy you a watch.'

It was the sort of joke they had begun to make, a residue of their wit. But she saw from his unchanging expression, the slight shift of his shoulder from hers, and his silence that he was annoyed. So she too fell silent and stared out of the window.

His annoyance went deeper than she imagined. It wasn't only the grotesque scene in the teashop, the sight of the men, both mountaineer and mouse, reduced to caricature. In the teashop he had been seized by a revulsion for all the women. For Miss Chichester, corseted and fat and flourishing, however distressed, however widowed. For the eater's keepers, gross in their cosiness. And the blushing little mute in soft colours he had hated most of all. The decorative little creeper would become the parasite; the keeper would become the kept, permitted to have his sayings, to perform his tricks.

For a fortnight, for twenty-four hours a day, except when he or she went to the bathroom, he and Margaret had been together. It was a new and disturbing experience. In the teashop this disturbance had reached its climax, and Margaret's playful sentence – 'I'll buy you a watch' – spoken in the tone of one encouraging a child, which was permissible in the circumstances (after the observation of something humorous in 'life'), had released all his resentment.

Yet mingled with this was the feeling that his thoughts about women and his marriage as they drove through the darkening countryside, where darkness still conveyed threat, were a betrayal of her who sat beside him, not at all fat, not at all parasitic, full only of loving, humiliating, killing concern.

Their silence, their quarrel, continued at the hotel, the desk-clerk noting their mood with satisfaction.

Towards the end of the evening, however, her presence, which at the teashop he had wished away, had developed, because of this very silence, into a comfort. When in bed he wilfully stimulated the return of that moment of hallucination in the white void, the loss of reality, his alarm was real, and he said, 'Doggie.'

'Doggie.'

Her own hardness had vanished. He could tell she had been crying.

4

It was on that night that the idea of the Knights Companion – the name came later and was the creation of young Whymper, the PRO – came to Mr Stone. The idea came suddenly when he was in bed, came whole, and to his surprise in the morning it was still good. All the way to London he turned it over in his mind, adding nothing, experiencing only the anxious joy of someone who fears that his creation may yet in some way elude him.

As soon as he got home he announced that he was going to 'work' in the study. Such an announcement had been long hoped for, and the two women hastened to supply his wants, Margaret's delight touched with relief that the silence she had noted all day was not moodiness. She adjusted the reading lamp, sharpened pencils; without being asked she took in a hot drink. Unwilling herself to withdraw, until she noticed Mr Stone's impatience, she gave instructions to Miss Millington that the Master was working and was not to be disturbed. Miss Millington compressed her lips and attempted to walk on tiptoe. Her long black skirts made it difficult to tell whether she was succeeding; but so she persevered, whispering in hoarse explosions that carried farther than her normal gasping speech.

While, in the study, aware only of the baize-covered desk (Margaret's) as a pool of light in the darkness, Mr Stone wrote, soft pencil running smoothly over crisp white paper.

Until late that night he worked. When he returned from the office on the following day he went directly to the study; and again it was announced that he was working. And so for more than a week it went on. He wrote, he corrected, he re-wrote; and fatigue never came to him. His handwriting changed. Losing its neatness, becoming cramped and crabbed, some of its loops wilfully inelegant, it yet acquired a more pleasing, more authoritative appearance, even a symmetry. The lines were straight; the margins made themselves. The steady patterning of each page was a joy, the scratch of soft pencil on receiving paper, the crossings out, the corrections in balloons in the margin.

And then the writing was finished. And though Mr Stone might go up in the evenings to the study, there was now nothing there to occupy him as before. The fair copy made, he put it in his briefcase one morning (giving that object a purpose at last), and took it out of the house to the office, where he persuaded one of the girls from the pool to type it. Two or three days later, receiving the typescript on rich Excal paper, he was struck anew by the perfection and inevitability of what he had written. And now he was overcome by shyness. He was unwilling to submit the typescript to the head of his department. He did not think he was a good advertisement for his work, and preferred it to be sent to someone who did not know him. This was why, ignoring correct procedure, he some days later adressed what he had written to Sir Harry, the head of Excal, enclosed a covering letter, and let the envelope fall into the Internal Post tray.

He felt exhausted, sad and empty. He might garden, watch television or read the newspapers: his evenings remained a blank.

He expected nothing to happen, but was not surprised when Keenan, from Accounts, a man who knew everything before it happened and took pleasure in making a secret of facts that were well known, came into the library one day and, negotiating the last steps to his desk on a ridiculous tiptoe, said in a whisper, 'I believe they'll be wanting you at Head Office, Stoney.'

Keenan didn't say more, but it was clear he believed that Mr Stone was guilty of a misdemeanour. His moustache curled up above his small well-shaped teeth; his eyes twinkled behind his spectacles with one arm missing (a dereliction he cultivated); within his baggy trousers his long, thin legs appeared to be twitching at the knees.

And quickly the word went round the office. Mr Stone was wanted at Head Office! As though Mr Stone had committed an offence of such enormity that the department was incapable of handling it and had passed it on to Head Office, resulting in the present summons, such as only the head of the department received.

Mr Stone was aware of the talk. He caught the looks. And he pretended to an indifference which he knew would be interpreted as an unexpected bravery. The situation was oddly familiar. Then he remembered the eater in the Cornwall teashop. 'Of course there was a lot of whispering. But what's so funny about a last day, I said.' This was unsettling. But the familiarity went deeper. All the events of the morning seemed to have been lived through before.

And it was only towards the end of the morning, when he was walking past Evans's open door, that he realized what it was. Evans was ex-R A F, a fact he never mentioned but which others invariably did. He wore dark-blue double-breasted suits, moved briskly on his short legs, leather heels giving each step a military sharpness, and he had the severe manner of an importantly busy man. He was suspect even when he descended among the 'boys', for he was a type of head-boy, a self-appointed office watch-dog who permitted himself jokes about superiors and office organization which on analysis could always be seen to be harmless but which occasionally encouraged some of the boys to be indiscreet. Walking, then, past the always open door of Evans, Mr Stone found himself carrying the needless papers which, to give himself the appearance of being busy, he carried whenever he left the library. And it occurred to him that on that day of all days the papers were not really necessary, that the look Evans, sitting frowning at his desk, gave him was not the everyday look, but the look of awe which he had been receiving from everyone that morning. And at last he was able to place the familiarity of the morning's happenings. What he felt now was the sensation he enjoyed in his fantasies when he flew calmly about in his armchair and the people in the office stared in astonishment.

So he exaggerated his calm, and it was only when he was on the train, the briefcase on his lap, that he relaxed. The delicate lines about his deep-set eyes became lines of humour; the lips curved. He smiled, a tired, elderly office worker oblivious of the crowd, his eyes fixed unseeing on the insurance poster.

After dinner that evening, when he was filling his pipe and Margaret was knitting, in light of painful dullness (she was sensitive to harsh light), he said, 'I believe they'll be wanting me at Head Office.'

The words meant little to her. And she simply said, 'That's very nice, Doggie.'

He fell silent. She did not notice it, so it did not develop into one of their silences. However, he resolved to tell her nothing more.

Old Harry – as he was known to those who did not know him, but Sir Harry to those whom he admitted to converse which they hoped to suggest was intimate – was a terrifying figure. In the eyes of their wives, men like Mr Stone and Tomlinson and Tomlinson's friends had their forbidding public image as well. But whereas they dropped the public mask in private, Old Harry, such was his importance, dropped his public mask in public. He wrote letters to *The Times*. He wrote on the number of pins in new shirts, the number of matches in matchboxes; he wrote on concrete lamp-standards. He never entered the first cuckoo competition, but he made important contributions to 'The Habits of the No. 11 Bus' and initiated the correspondence on the London Transport bus ticket. ('The smudged curling scrap of paper with which I am presented neither looks nor feels like an omnibus ticket, which is after all a certificate of travel, however humdrum. It is scarcely suitable for tucking into the hatband, like any respectable ticket. Rather, its flimsiness and general disreputable appearance encourage one heedlessly to crumple it into a ball or, in more creative moments, neatly to fold it into a miniature accordion, both ball and accordion vanishing at the moment when the omnibus inspector makes a request for their appearance.') Transport was in fact his special subject, and he had built up a reputation, nowhere more formidable than at Excal, for his knowledge of the country's railway system. (What he said to Miss Menzies at the garden party was famous. 'So you live in Streatham? But that's where the main line trains branch off for Portsmouth.') Every letter Old Harry wrote to *The Times* was cut out by Miss Menzies together with the correspondence contents column, which made the title of the writer plain, pasted on to a sheet of thin white paper and circulated round the department, returning from its round impressively initialled in a variety of handwritings, inks and pencils. The effect of these frivolous letters over the years was to turn Old Harry into a figure of awe. With every letter he receded; his occasional references to himself as 'a member of the travelling public' were shattering; and the impression of grandeur and inaccessibility was completed by his reported left-wing leanings.

So Mr Stone's departure for his interview with Old Harry at Head Office, for a reason neither Evans nor anyone else in the department knew, was in the nature of a solemn send-off. He was in his best Simpson's suit; Margaret, with an appreciation of Sir Harry rather than the occasion, had chosen his tie. For a moment Mr Stone felt it was like going to a wedding, and the feeling was encouraged by the tearful appearance in the library of one of the typists, a broad-framed young slattern whose main topic of conversation was the refusal of the LCC to put her down on their housing list (in fact she and her husband ran a car). She had had a difficult morning; shc had been 'reprimanded' by Evans; and now she said almost angrily to Mr Stone, 'It's people like you who make it hard for the rest of us.'

He paid no attention and, walking down the middle of the corridor, not at the side, as he had done in the past to escape detection, and carrying no papers in his hand, went out of the office, in the middle of the workday morning.

He had hardly sat down in his chair in the library that afternoon when Keenan came tiptoeing in.

'Well, what did Old Harry have to say?' Keenan's knees were twitching; his hands, in his pockets, appeared to be fondling his private parts; and the concern in his whispered question was belied by the delight in his eyes, his lips, his moustache.

'Sir Harry and I,' Mr Stone said, 'discussed a project I had put up for the creation of a new department.'

And again Mr Stone had the delicious sensation of flying in his chair. Keenan's reaction was a caricature of astonishment and incredulity. For seconds he held himself in his conspiratorial stoop, held his smile. Then he straightened, his hands and knees went still, his smile grew empty and disappeared, and it was as if the distance between the two men had become unbridgeable. Keenan's joviality vanished. The lines of good humour in his face became fussy lines of worry and suppressed hysteria. In his thin, shapeless trousers, his broken spectacles, he appeared, beside Mr Stone in his Simpson's suit, quite abject and mean. The almost immediate return of his restless jollity did not efface that moment.

Another relationship had been adjusted, changed. But Mr Stone flew. For the rest of that afternoon, for the rest of that week, he walked about the corridors of the office as one who sat in his chair and flew.

At the end of the month Mr Stone was moved to Welfare, to a new office in a new building, where the furniture was brand-new from Heal's and where there was no Miss Menzies to signal the passing of the days by her costume. His salary was raised to £1,500 a year. His transfer but not his salary was mentioned in the house magazine; there was also a photograph. And it was the house magazine that he casually showed Margaret on the day of its publication (some half a dozen copies in his briefcase), saying, 'Something about me here.'

Around him the world was awakening to green and sun. The tree in the school grounds at the back became flecked, then brushed, with green. And this was no mere measuring of time. He was at one with the tree, for with it he developed from day to day, and every day there were new and inspiring things to do. At Welfare there were the long sessions with Whymper, the young PRO who had been assigned to the new department. The idea, Whymper said, was good, very good. He was 'excited' by it, but it had to be 'licked into shape'. These last words he spoke with almost physical relish, passing a thick tongue over his top lip, tapping a cigarette in his own manner on his silver cigarette case. Whymper saw himself as a processer of raw material. He spoke as one whose chief delight lay in sifting, cleaning, removing impurities. He said he made nothing. 'But,' he added, 'I make something out of nothing.'

For someone who took pride in his ability to refine, his appearance was strangely coarse, and Mr Stone's first impressions were not good. The squarish jaws were slack and a little too fleshy, the lips bruised-looking with rims like welts (having tapped his cigarette in that way of which he was so proud, he rolled it between these lips, and sometimes the cigarette came out wet at the end); the eyes were soft and brown and unreliable, as of someone made uncertain by suffering. He was of medium height and average physique. For such men ready-to-wear suits are made by the hundred thousand, but nothing Whymper wore appeared to fit. His clothes had the slackness of his jaw; they suggested that the flesh below was soft, never exposed, unhardened. His jacket, always awry, made him look round-shouldered and sometimes even humped. And his fancy waistcoats – for Whymper was interested in clothes – were only startling and ridiculous.

Mr Stone did not like being told that his idea had to be licked into shape. And his displeasure grew when at their first meeting in Welfare Whymper abruptly said,

'I hope you don't mind my saying so, Stone, but I find the way you tap a cigarette profoundly irritating.'

Cigarette in hand, Mr Stone paused.

'Go on,' Whymper said. 'Let's see you tap it.'

Mr Stone held the cigarette between forefinger and thumb and struck.

This, Whymper said, was wrong. The correct way was to let the cigarette drop from a height of half an inch, so that it bounced back into the grip of forefinger and thumb.

For two or three minutes they tapped cigarettes, Whymper the instructor, Mr Stone the pupil.

Distaste for Whymper was, however, quickly replaced by pleasure in the man's quick mind, his capacity for hard work and above all his enthusiasm, which Mr Stone took as a compliment to himself, though it very soon became clear that Whymper's 'excitement' differed from his own.

'How about this?' Whymper said. 'Our pensioners visit the pensioners of clients. Take them a little gift from the company and so on. It wouldn't break Excal. And look. Word will get around. "Our relationships are more than business relationships. They are relationships between friends".' He spoke the words as if they were already a slogan. 'That sort of thing will do a lot more good than all those Christmas cards. Nobody likes a PRO. You don't have to tell me. But who will suspect these old boys? And think. Men working for Excal even after they retire. A whole army of Excal old boys on the march, in every corner of the country.'

Mr Stone allowed himself to play with the idea. He gave the pensioners of his fantasy long white beards, thick, knotted sticks and Chelsea Hospital uniforms. He saw them tramping about country lanes, advancing shakily through gardens in full bloom, and knocking on the doors of thatched cottages.

'Thousands of unpaid PROs,' Whymper was saying. 'Welcome wherever they go. One in every village.'

'Unrealistic.'

Always there was this difference in their approaches,

Whymper talking of benefits to Excal, Mr Stone having to conceal that his plan had not been devised to spread the fame of Excal, but simply for the protection of the old.

And in Whymper's attitude lay this especial irritant, that he seemed not to acknowledge the concern and fear out of which the plan had arisen, or the passion which had supported Mr Stone during its elaboration, going up night after night to his study. Whymper did not acknowledge this; Mr Stone was unwilling to state it. And as they endlessly discussed modifications and alternatives Mr Stone found that he was beginning, however slightly, to adopt Whymper's position that the venture was one of public relations.

'I am excited by this thing,' Whymper said every day during their discussions. 'I feel that something big can be made of it.'

He was full of ideas. It amused him to exercise his inventiveness, and he described even the wildest idea at length, with much tangential detail. When these ideas ran down or were otherwise disposed of, he returned to the duplicated memorandum that lay before him and asked Mr Stone to outline his scheme afresh.

'We write to our pensioners,' Mr Stone said. 'We invite those who want to do so to become Visitors or Companions. In this way we sort out the active from the inactive. We send our Visitors or Companions or whatever we call them details of the people they have to visit. The inactive. Age, department, date of retirement, length of service and so on.'

'That's where we'll need staff,' Whymper said.

'Our Visitors report cases of special need. We investigate those. But for the normal visit nothing more is required than the Visitor's travelling expenses and a refund for the small gift – flowers or chocolate – that he takes. In this way we organize our pensioners into a self-sufficient, self-help unit. All we provide is the administration.'

Always they came back like this to Mr Stone's original points, so that it seemed that by 'licking into shape'

Whymper meant only wandering away from a point before returning to it.

This perversity of Whymper's encouraged Mr Stone to speak with increasing enthusiasm. Fear of being too explicit about his motives led him to vagueness. But he steadily revealed more of what he truly felt, and to his surprise Whymper neither derided nor looked puzzled.

'This is interesting,' Whymper would say intently, his eyes narrowing. 'You are holding me. This is what I want.'

Mr Stone expanded. He had solved some of the problems of old age. He rescued men from inactivity; he protected them from cruelty. He preserved for men the comradeship of the office, which released them from the confinement of family relationships. He kept alive loyalty to the company. And he did all this at almost no cost: his scheme would cost Excal no more than £20,000 a year.

'A society,' Whymper said, 'for the protection of the impotent male.'

Whymper's talk was full of sexual references like this. Mr Stone had learned to ignore them, but at this remark he could not hide his embarrassment and disgust.

Whymper was delighted. 'This is what I want,' he said. 'You've got me interested. Go on.'

More and more, in the process of licking into shape, Whymper placed Mr Stone in the position of the defender, the explainer, until at length, passion exhausted, Mr Stone was driven to make easy statements which were like insincerities. But these impressed Whymper no less.

Once, towards the end of the week, Mr Stone heard himself saying, 'It is a way, you see, of helping the poor old people.'

It was ridiculous and cheap, and far from what he felt. But Whymper only said in an earnest, matter-of-fact way, 'The treatment of the old in this country is scandalous.'

And it was at this level that their discussions remained, as though they had both decided not to open their minds fully and had tacitly agreed not to point this out to one another.

They came to discuss the name of the project.

'We want something really inspiring,' Whymper said. 'Something that will actually get the old boys out on the road and up to the various front doors.'

Mr Stone had not thought of a name at all. And now, sitting at the desk with Whymper, Whymper tapping his cigarette and rolling it between his lips, he felt he did not want to think of a name. He feared a further cheapening of his idea.

'Luncheon Vouchers are big business,' Whymper said. 'And you know why? The name. Luncheon voucher. In those words you have lunch, crunch, munch, mouth, rich. You even have belch. Why, the words are like a rich meal. That's what we want. Something that would explain. Something that would inspire. Something memorable.'

'Veterans,' Mr Stone said.

Whymper shook his head tolerantly. 'Just what we don't want. The name we want will suggest youth. Youth and comradeship and the protection of the male.'

Mr Stone thought he saw how Whymper processed his raw material.

'Something like Knights,' Whymper said.

'Scarcely for the protection of the male.'

Whymper paid no attention. 'Knights of the something. Knights of the open road. Knights-errant. That's just what they're going to be, aren't they? Knights-errant.'

Mr Stone thought the suggestion ridiculous. He felt like sweeping the Heal's table clear of memoranda and paper, saying something offensive to Whymper, and returning to the peace of his library desk.

There was silence, while Mr Stone inwardly raged and Whymper thought. Then, as sometimes happened when he thought, Whymper grew lightheaded.

'Door-knockers,' he said. 'The Company's Door-Knockers. The Most Worshipful Company of Door-Knockers.'

Mr Stone lit a cigarette, tapping it in his own way and

rather hard. But the suggestion went home. He stripped his pensioners of their red uniforms and gave them elaborate ones in dark brown with yellow stripes; they wore knee breeches and black stockings and knocked on doors with poles carved with some meaningful ancient design.

'The Knight Visitors,' Whymper said.

'That's another sort of night.'

'I am not a child, Stone.'

'You're behaving like one.'

Whymper's uncertain eyes went appealing. 'The Good Companions.'

'Knight Companions,' Mr Stone said wearily.

'Scarcely at their age.' Whymper gave a little titter.

Mr Stone looked at the window.

'Knights Companion,' Whymper said.

Mr Stone was silent.

'Right in every way,' Whymper said. 'Youth in the Knight. The Company in Companion. And then the association with those titles. KCVO and something else. Knight Companion of the something. Suggesting age and dignity. So we have youth and age, dignity and good companionship. *And* the Company. Knights Companion. God! The thing is full of possibilities. Your Knights Companion can form a Knights' Circle. A Round Table. They can have a dinner every year. They can have competitions. You know, Stone, I believe we've licked this thing into shape.'

And now Margaret took on a new role, and took it on as easily as she had always taken on new roles. She ceased to be merely the wife who waited for her husband at home; she became the wife who encouraged and inspired her husband in his work. Whereas before the nature of Mr Stone's employment was scarcely mentioned, a little of the fraudulence of the designation of 'head librarian' remaining to remind them both of their spurious attitudes at their first meeting, now they talked about his work incessantly, and the subject of his retirement receded. Her dress subtly changed: when she welcomed Mr Stone in the evenings she might also without disgrace have received visitors. (And what affection he had begun to feel for her clothes, for the garnets and the red dress of watered silk, once the arresting attributes of a new person, now the familiar, carefully looked-after parts of a limited wardrobe.) She still moulded herself around him, but she expanded, regaining something of her earlier manner. She saw, before Mr Stone did, that her responsibilities had widened, and she spoke of these responsibilities as of a bother which yet had to be squarely faced. She spoke of 'entertaining' as of an imminent and awful possibility; and she became graver and more insistent as the references to Mr Stone and the Knights Companion became more frequent, longer and self-congratulatory in the house magazine. Duty called her, called them both; and duty must not be shirked.

So then, like any young couple (as Margaret herself said, laughing to counter ridicule and destroy embarrassment), they discussed the changes that had to be made in the house. They needed new carpets, new pictures, new wallpaper, and Margaret was full of suggestions. Mr Stone listened with only half a mind, saying little, savouring Margaret's feminine talk in that room with the tigerskin as part of his new situation. His gestures became more leisured; he exaggerated them, acting them out for his own pleasure. The reading of the evening paper was no longer the exercise of a habit which solaced and without which the evening was incomplete. It was with a delicious sense of patronage that he read about the rest of the wonderful world. He was more easily amused and more easily touched. He often read items out to Margaret; and it was a relief, so tight were they with emotion, to laugh or be moved. Every sensation was heightened. They even fabricated little quarrels, which they never, however, allowed to develop into one of their silences.

About the improvements to the house Mr Stone said little. Playfully adopting her attitude, he said that these things were for the woman; just as she, in spite of all Mr Stone's expositions, pretended to know little about the

Knights Companion and at times even claimed to be slightly bored or irritated by all the talk about them.

So gradually the house began to change again. Gradually, because it was discovered that if the repairs were to be thorough whole areas of the house would have to be rebuilt. Part of the roof had subsided, the attic floor was dangerous, the window frames had buckled. Uncompensated war damage, Mr Stone said – he told her how the planes came over this part of South London every Saturday night – and it roused Margaret to perfect fury against the government. They decided, therefore, to do up only those sections which might be exposed to the view of distinguished guests: the hall, the sitting-room, the dining-room, the bathroom, and those parts of the stairs which were visible from the highest stage of ascent that might reasonably be considered legitimate. The kitchen, on the ground floor, and their own bedroom, on the first, they decided to leave untouched.

Miss Millington was thought to be competent to undertake the redecorating. First of all she painted. Her fussy, ineffectual and inaccurate brush marks were to be seen everywhere. She proclaimed herself thereafter ready for the papering, hinting at the same time at the availability of Eddie and Charley, who, she said, were just finishing the fish shop. And that very afternoon a neat white card – E. Beeching and C. Bryant, Builders and Decorators – came into the letter box. They called that evening. They were elderly but spry. Bryant, round-faced and with spectacles, smiled. Beeching, the cadaverous-faced spokesman, said they were freelances, anxious to build up a reputation. Their prices were high; but Beeching said the prices of the firm they had previously worked for were higher. They were engaged. And gradually, section by section, one patch of building and decorating separated from the other by a week or a fortnight, during which Beeching and Bryant went off to do other jobs and Miss Millington was encouraged to try her hand again, the public areas of the house, or the areas soon to be public, were done.

Margaret had envisaged dinner parties spreading out

on to the lawn in summer. It was a small lawn, and in spite of views of the backs of houses might have been suitable, particularly with the openness of the adjacent school grounds. But the neighbours were not co-operative. The keeper of the black cat was no handyman; his fence was in an appalling condition, wobbling and sagging; and his garden was rank, with a few hollyhocks and overgrown rose trees rising out of much bush. The people on the other side went in for desert rather than jungle; they also took in lodgers, and their back garden was strung with clothes lines. Their own back fence, too, was not what it might have been, being steadily forced out of true by the roots of the tree Mr Stone considered every day when shaving.

So the changes that came to the house did not alter its character. To the alien mustiness brought in by Margaret's possessions, which had now grown familiar, there was added only a gloss. The redecorated portions of the house did not lose their smell of old dirt, rags and polish. And every evening when they climbed up the stairs to their bedroom, to the brown velvet curtains, the tasselled lampshade painted green, the nondescript carpet and linoleum, it was like re-entering the old house, the past.

Change also came to Miss Millington. Whereas before she was an old servant whose inefficiency and physical failings were getting more and more troublesome, now she became precious; she added lustre to the establishment. In how many houses these days were front doors opened by uniformed maids? And now to summon her, who had previously only been shouted or ullulated for, there appeared, on the table in the hall, next to the flowerpot in the brass vase, a brass bell on a brass tray; and to enable her to summon them, there appeared at the same time on the wall a large gong of beaten brass, which the failing old soul managed with great difficulty, compressing her lips, closing her eyes, and striking in a daze with a slow curving gesture until the sound she created penetrated her consciousness and reminded her to stop. So now she existed in the changed house, shuffling steadily in and out of her roles as drudge and ornament, a pensioner only on Thursdays, when she went to the pensioners' cinema show to sleep through the afternoon.

'All we provide is the administration,' Mr Stone had told Whymper, and now they were occupied with the administering of the pilot scheme. So Whymper called it. He had a flair for urgent, important names. It was his suggestion that the Knights Companion Department of Welfare should be called a 'Unit'. The Unit was conducting an 'operation', for which it needed 'intelligence'. This accumulation of military metaphor, combined with the frequency with which Whymper called him by his name and referred to the large-scale wall-map of the area chosen for the pilot scheme, occasionally led Mr Stone to indulge in the fantasy that they were both in general's uniform, in a high panelled room such as Mr Stone had seen in some films: they spoke softly, but at their word pensioners deployed all over the country.

He relished Whymper's words. He relished the urgency Whymper, by his manner, his bulging briefcase and his talk of paperwork as of something tedious but vitally important, gave to the operation. He relished the words 'administration' and 'staff'. And staff was recruited, the word and the concept declining into three typists whose ordinariness and near-illiteracy robbed them of the charm of typists in films and cartoons (which, in spite of his experience, was what he expected), four male clerks whose advanced age diminished and somehow mocked the urgency of the project and whose appearance of unremitting diligence went with a strangely limited output, and a junior accountant from Yorkshire, a young man of ridiculous sartorial and social pretensions.

Letters had to be written, replies sorted, Knights Companion appointed, short biographies of the inactive prepared, machinery set up for the handling of accounts. And in spite of the staff, diligently tapping, diligently turning over pages, bustling about corridors with sheaves of paper, a good deal of this work had to be done by Mr

Stone himself. At the same time a continuous stream of propaganda on behalf of the project had to be maintained. This was Whymper's job. And Mr Stone was grateful for Whymper. Whymper had flair. All the ideas which had seemed theatrical and cheap were those that caught on.

It was Whymper's idea that a Knight Companion should be issued with a scroll of appointment on hand-made paper with rough edges. For this words had to be composed, archaic but not whimsical, and authoritative; and Whymper composed them. A special visit had to be made to Sir Harry to get his approval for the use of the Excal seal on the scrolls, and to Mr Stone's surprise Sir Harry was not annoyed or amused by their play, but enthusiastic and commending. It was Whymper's idea that Knights Companion should carry in their lapels little silver figures of knights, armoured and visored, charging at full gallop, lances tilted – that and nothing else, no word or letter. It was his further idea, though this was not adopted, that all Excal pensioners should wear little metal roses, of varying colours to indicate their length of service with the Company, to facilitate recognition by other pensioners and by Knights Companion. And so always Whymper's mind sparked, racing ahead of the Unit's schedule and occasionally wasting much time thereby (for days, for example, he played with the design of the charging knight, though he was no artist), but always generating enthusiasm.

And by his work of administration, of creating out of an idea – words written on paper in his study – an organization of real people, Mr Stone never ceased to be thrilled. Now his worn, shiny briefcase carried documents that mattered. Now, too, he caught himself looking at briefcases in shop windows, ready to discard the once fraudulent container that had given him so much pleasure in the days when the weeks were to be got through and numbered and hoarded. His talk became exclusively of the Knights Companion. Margaret knew as well as anyone of the problems of staff, and Grace Tomlinson responded with tales of staff problems that Tomlinson had silently endured for years. Now,

Grace seemed to say, she could speak: Margaret and Richard could understand. And Margaret gave a ready retrospective sympathy.

The pilot scheme ran into certain difficulties.

A former head of an Excal department, scenting old blood on his appointment as a Knight Companion, took a leisurely tour through Wales, visited eight widely scattered pensioners of his acquaintance, and sent in a bill for £249 17s 5½d, neatly worked out, the bills of expensive hotels enclosed together with restaurant bills, garage bills and receipts for the gifts he had bought. For one pensioner he had bought a radio. He regretted his inability to buy a television set for another, who had gone deaf; and in his letter strongly urged the Unit to do so.

Twenty Knights Companion were on the road. Letters were hastily dispatched to nineteen. And the bill of the former department head, rejected in horror by official after higher official, had to go up to Sir Harry himself. It was decided to refund the sum demanded; but with the cheque went a letter, composed after much labour by Whymper and Mr Stone, outlining the limited scope of the project. A Knight Companion, the letter said, was not expected unduly to exert himself; he was to visit only those pensioners – and they were within easy reach – whose names were supplied to him; and only token gifts were to be made. Energy such as the former department head had displayed was admirable, but for eight visits he was entitled to no more than £4, and they could not hide from him that his request for more than sixty times that sum had gravely embarrassed them with their accountants and threatened the continuance of the scheme itself.

Promptly the reply came, in a large envelope: the scroll of appointment was inside. In a long confused letter, indignant and hurt and apologetic, the former department head thanked the Unit and Excal for the cheque. But, he said, he felt obliged to return the scroll of appointment. In his day he encouraged his staff to believe, as he himself was encouraged, that Excal did a thing well or not at all. As for the silver pin, he was keeping that for the time being; he awaited their instructions.

They urged him to keep the pin. And nothing more was heard from him until the end of the year.

Less disastrous, though perhaps more embarrassing, was the administrative error which sent an inadequately briefed Knight Companion, a former messenger, to visit a retired Excal director. The short biography provided was democratically defective and the messenger knew nothing of the eminence of the person he journeyed to succour. Pertinacious in the face of kindly surprise, his chivalry at last turned to doubt and then was dissipated in anxiety. The former director appeared; the messenger bowed low, presented a packet of Co-op tea, and withdrew.

Whymper had made much in his handouts of having a messenger and a department head as Knights Companion. But now they decided that there ought to be some parity between the visitor and the visited. It was also decided to abandon the fixed gift allowance for a sliding scale related to the status of the person visited. It was, too, at this time, disillusionment with the Knights Companion momentarily going deep, that the Yorkshire accountant suggested that bills for gifts should be sent direct to the Unit. This would mean more work, but the accountant produced some figures to show that if as a result of this precaution two or three shillings were saved per visit – and it might be more, for some shops could be persuaded to give Excal a discount – the Unit would gain or at worst break even.

'What we need,' he said, 'is more staff.'

The request for more staff, enthusiastically put up by Whymper and Mr Stone, was as enthusiastically greeted by Sir Harry. And more staff was recruited, so that the female flurry towards the lavatories between twelve-thirty and one and five and five-thirty became disturbing: tock-tock-tock on brisk heels, pause, flush, tock-tock-tock: like a lazy sea whipped to spasmodic but towering fury on a steep rocky shore.

Two further irregularities came to light, and to the first there appeared to be no solution. A series of aggrieved complaining letters in various shaky hands revealed that a Knight Companion was using his right of entry to homes to propagate the creed of the Jehovah's Witnesses. The gifts he took, and for which the Unit had been paying for some weeks, were copies of *Let God Be True* and an annual subscription to a magazine called *Awake!* Eighteen letters were hastily dispatched, warning the Knights Companion against such practices, and to the Witness himself there went a letter informing him that he was struck off the roll of Knights Companion. A calm reply was received. The Witness wrote that what he had done was legitimate, since the truth had to be spread by whatever means. Authority always feared the truth and the action of the Unit did not surprise him; but he would continue with his 'preaching and publishing work'. He carried out his threat, and for long the district remained disturbed, as could be seen from the concentration of red on the wall-map, where blue pins indicated satisfaction, red dissatisfaction, and yellow cases to be investigated by the Unit itself.

It was decided that in future Knights Companion would be carefully sounded for the depth of their religious convictions. More work was involved, because Personnel did not have the necessary information. And Whymper, saying it in much the same way as he used to say, 'The treatment of the old in this country is scandalous', said, 'That's the terrible thing about living in a pagan country.' (This was Mr Stone's first intimation that Whymper might be a Roman Catholic.) 'A man works forty, fifty years for a firm, and no one cares whether he is Muslim or Buddhist.'

The other irregularity was discovered by chance. A Knight Companion claimed to have visited ten persons in his area, and was sent £5. The very day the cheque was sent, however, Pensions reported that one of the pensioners had moved to another address a fortnight before the date mentioned by the Knight Companion. Investigation revealed that the pensioner had not been visited at all. A further stern letter was sent, a further set of insignia recalled, and Whymper decreed that in every list of pensioners sent out thereafter to Knights Companion one dead pensioner should be included.

At the dinner parties they had begun to give – the guests senior officials from Welfare, Personnel and Pensions, Miss Millington despairingly praised by her mistress for her chips and her fish – these were the stories that Margaret and Mr Stone told. They had thought their life's store of stories completed; now they had the joy of acquiring new stories almost every week. The story of the cat and the cheese, through which Mr Stone and the Tomlinsons had sat so often, was forgotten, almost as completely as the cat: the animal had ceased to dig up the garden, which Mr Stone on free evenings and on weekends diligently cultivated, with the now superfluous but still reverential encouragement of Margaret and Miss Millington.

To some of these dinners Whymper came. He astonished them the first time by appearing in formal wear, his jacket sitting uncomfortably as always on his soft round shoulders. At the first meeting he was excessively courtly towards Margaret, and displayed none of the brusqueness or desire to shock which Mr Stone had feared. He was courtly, but he was severe. His eyes were narrowed; his mouth determinedly set, giving an unconvincing tightness to his jaw. He smoked innumerable cigarettes, tapping them in his way and rolling them slowly between his lips. He said little. He resisted all Margaret's brightness, and she was intimidated by him. She thought she had failed with Whymper, and so did Mr Stone. But he came again, and again, accepting each invitation with alacrity; and each time he appeared in formal clothes. Margaret persevered in her brightness, and gradually Whymper thawed, acquiring something of his office manner. He sprawled in his chair, his legs wide apart, his back humped; his eyes lost their severity and uncertainty; and he occasionally gave that titter which Mr Stone found coarse and irritating in the office but which he was now glad to hear in his home.

'Tell me, Mr Whymper,' Margaret said one evening, in her best imitation of the actress, 'what do you think of all this talk about virgin birth?'

'What they call virgin birth I call grudge birth,' Whymper said. 'Somebody had it in for the husband.'

Margaret saw it before Mr Stone. She forgot the actress, her mouth went square with delight, and she gave a great guffawing laugh, widening her knees and leaning towards Whymper.

Their friendship grew firm. He became a regular visitor to the house and often had dinner alone with them, so that at times Mr Stone wondered whether Whymper, in spite of his smart, busy appearance, had no other friends. In his usual way of not letting civility stand in the way of honesty, Whymper spoke his mind about Margaret's clothes and the food she offered. Mr Stone suffered, but Margaret was delighted. It was 'just like Whymper'. This recognition pleased him, and he made an effort to please. He became Bill to Margaret, and she Margaret to him, while Mr Stone remained simply Stone, spoken in a mock-formal, affectionate way at home, seriously at the office.

Sometimes Olive and Gwen were among the guests. Gwen was as sour-sweet as ever. But she had been slimming – it showed in the slight looseness of skin about her neck – and she had at last managed to impose some shape on her body. She wore her brassières tight, so that her large breasts were pushed upwards. They impended; they dominated. But they were shapely, and she was not without attraction when she was seated. When she stood up the impression was spoilt. For her hips were wide, and though not disproportionately so, the foolish child, in an effort to emphasize her breasts, wore tight-waisted dresses and sometimes broad belts which exaggerated the broadness of her hips.

Gwen was always a strain, and so now Mr Stone began to find Olive. He wanted her admiration, but he thought her only tepid. In spite of all the show of friendship, the exclamations at this new decoration and that, in spite of the ease with which she and Margaret spoke, it was as if Olive had withdrawn from the household, and could no longer fully participate in its joys or sadness. Even when Margaret was out of the room she spoke as if Margaret were still there. And Mr Stone was disappointed. He expected something sweeter and more conspiratorial.

The leaves on the tree in the school grounds faded and fell, revealing once more the houses of the Monster and the Male (ferreting this autumn into the earth for a purpose which Mr Stone in spite of long observation could not ascertain). The pilot scheme ran its course and could be pronounced a success. Impressive sums had been spent; but the achievements were impressive. The Unit had been licked into shape. Administration had been simplified, liaison with Pensions and other departments regularized; and expansion could be easy. The usefulness of the scheme had been proved beyond doubt. The Knights Companion not only uncovered cases of distress and need; they also uncovered many cases of neglect and cruelty. Whymper fell on these with zeal, wrote them up in *Oyez! Oyez!*, the Unit's cyclostyled newsletter, and reproduced photographs of the Knights Companion concerned, encouraging the others to a more rigorous investigation of their charges. The protective function of the Unit became increasingly important, beyond what Whymper or even Mr Stone had envisaged. And the name of the Knights Companion, in which Mr Stone had at first discerned only Whymper's irreverence and professional enthusiasm, though Whymper always spoke it with the utmost earnestness and had indeed once roundly abused the junior accountant for speaking it with a smile of complicity, the name of the Knights Companion became a reality. For the operation had become a crusade.

It was another example of Whymper's flair, and Mr Stone was admiring. And such was Whymper's zeal, so great his delight at proofs of the scheme's usefulness, that Mr Stone could not be sure that Whymper had not committed himself without reserve to the cause. It was hard to tell with Whymper. In this respect he was a little like Evans, ex-RAF. He permitted himself moments of mockery, particularly at the petty crookedness which came to light, but he was quick to snub anyone, even Mr Stone, who attempted to do likewise. So that there were occasions when Mr Stone felt that he, absorbed in administration, and Whymper, speaking with the accents of passion, had exchanged roles.

'The thing's a success,' Whymper said, looking at the map with its blue pins everywhere, its obstinate patch of red, and its now liberal sprinkling of yellow. 'But what is success? We have a lot of letters, we can quote a lot of figures, the Knights are as happy as sandboys. But it isn't enough, Stone. A rescue here and a rescue there is all very well. But in a few months even that will become routine. Everyone will become bored, even the Knights. We want something big. Something explosive. Something that will drive the whole thing along on its steam for a year or so.'

This was Whymper, dissatisfied with a thing as soon as it began to run smoothly, needing the stimulus of fresh ideas, and always slightly unsettling to Mr Stone, who was content but not surprised at the proofs of the usefulness of his project, and whose delight in the creation of the Unit was doubled by its smooth functioning and the daily contemplation of real men and women, with serious lives of their own, engaged in the working out of a project he had sketched in words, in the pool of light in his study.

Then they discovered the Prisoner of Muswell Hill.

Late one afternoon Mr Stone received a telephone call from a man who announced himself as Mr Duke. Mr Duke was distracted and much of what he said was unintelligible. But Mr Stone gathered that Mr Duke had been recently appointed a Knight Companion, that he had on that day sported the silver knight on his lapel for the first time and gone out to pay his visits. The first two pensioners he called on were dead, and had been dead for years.

'I bought a walnut cake for them,' he said repeatedly, as though distressed by its perishable quality.

One of the pensioners was indeed dead. But Pensions reported that the other was alive, or that at any rate pensions were still being sent to him. A yellow button went up like a quarantine flag over Muswell Hill, and an investigator was sent out the next morning. She returned just before lunch, quite shaken, and told this story.

The address had turned out to be in one of the respectable redbrick streets of Muswell Hill. The house was not noticeable if one walked past it quickly, for red brick is red brick and there are more rank gardens in Muswell Hill than the borough of Hornsey would care to admit. It was only on scrutiny that one noticed that the house was derelict, the window frames washed of all paint, that the curtains had a curious colourlessness, and that about the structure there was that air of decay which comes from an absence of habitation. The walk up to the front door had strengthened that impression. The bells were rusted; so was the knocker. She had knocked and knocked. At length there was movement, and as soon as the door was opened she was assailed by the smell of dirt and mustiness and cats and rags, which came partly from the house and partly from the cheap fur coat that the woman who opened was wearing. This woman was about fifty, of medium height, with pale-blue eyes behind pink-framed spectacles. Her eyes were searching but held no suspicion. Behind her in the dark hallway there was continuous movement, and she held the door as much to prevent the escape of what was behind her as to deny entry to the investigator. The movement continued, little rubbings, bristlings, soft thumps. The house was full of cats. Her father, the woman said, was dead. She had already told them he was dead. Why did they want to hear it again?

The investigator forced her way into the hall. Cats rubbed against her legs, and to the protests of the woman in the fur coat she responded with something like bullying. There were many letters in the hall: a mound of football coupons, letters from various government departments, and all the literature the Knights Companion Unit had sent out. Breathing with difficulty, the investigator had searched the house, and in a room bolted from the outside had found her pensioner. The smell was even more disagreeable than that downstairs. The man did not see her; the room was in darkness; he was lying on a bed of rags. 'He doesn't like cats,' the woman in the fur coat said. The man appeared to have lost the gift of speech; what he uttered were gruff little noises. The investigator pulled down curtains, an easy task; with greater difficulty she opened windows. And then at last the man spoke, a sentence of pure foolishness. But here the investigator broke down and sobbed.

What did the man say, from the mound of rags on the bed?

'Going to put you up for the MCC.'

The story shocked and frightened Mr Stone. It awakened all the unease which he had lost sight of since joining Welfare, which he had submerged in the creation of the Unit, in the thrill of authorship and the savouring of his good fortune.

It was not one of the stories he told Margaret. And it was no consolation that evening to be in his own brightened home, where everything spoke of newness and the possibility of rapid change, where the bedroom with the green lamp-shade could become a prison. Its mustiness was again unfamiliar and threatening.

He was glad when morning came and he could get away to the office.

From his gloom he was rescued by Whymper, on whom the story of the Prisoner of Muswell Hill – as the newspapers later called the affair – had had an altogether stimulating effect. He too was shocked and horrified, but his fury was translated into energy, into a desire, as he said, 'to shame the country which permits this sort of thing to happen'.

'This is too big and disgraceful for *Oyez! Oyez!*,' he said. 'I think we should call in the Press.'

Mr Stone wished to dissociate himself from Whymper's zeal. He saw the advantages of publicity, but at the same time he feared, as he had feared the previous evening to reveal anything to Margaret, to publicize a humiliation which was so close to them all, a humiliation which rendered the threatened more vulnerable.

But he didn't say this. He only said, what Whymper expected him to say, 'I think we should move cautiously. I think this is a matter for higher authority.'

And Whymper agreed, not as one who had had an unexpectedly easy success but as one who out of deference and a desire for harmony was accepting a brake on his enthusiasm.

Once again it was as though unspoken words lay between them.

Higher authority was approached; higher authority was approving; and the story was given to the Press. In this way the Knights Companion scheme came to the notice of the public. The story was released in time for the Sundays, and there was enough interest for follow-up stories to appear in the dailies, national and provincial. The local Muswell Hill paper, whose posters, while photographers and reporters were in the area, proclaimed nothing more exciting than 'Boy, 11, Bitten by Alsatian', had solider fare for its readers.

In the commendations that followed, both from within Excal and without, Mr Stone found himself rejoicing. The Unit had established itself; its future was assured; the crusade would go on. He fended off congratulations by saying they had had a lot of luck. Whymper said as much. And Mr Stone revealed to Tomlinson and Tomlinson's friends the high-level discussions that had taken place before they had 'released the story' – speaking the words as one who had earned the right to speak them – to the Press.

Some time later Mr Stone travelled north on business. He took the opportunity to visit the Yorkshire asylum, called a hospital, where the daughter of the Prisoner of Muswell Hill was lodged. The Prisoner himself had died shortly after his release. The daughter had been freed of her fur coat and cats. She missed neither. She was entirely harmless and was allowed to look after the room of one of the doctors. Every morning she presented him with a bouquet of flowers from the hospital gardens. Every day she bought two sweets from the canteen. One she kept for herself, the other for a person she was unwilling to name. For this person she looked all morning. She did not find him. Then sadly she gave the sweet to the staff nurse.

5

With this success there came a change in Mr Stone's attitude to Whymper. Nothing was said, and their relationship continued as before, but Mr Stone found himself more and more reassessing Whymper. He found himself studying Whymper's face and mannerisms, attempting to see them as if for the first time, and he wondered how he had come to suppress his initial distaste, how he had managed to feel affection for Whymper, to enjoy his obscene laugh and obscene jokes (Whymper on the types of fart, Whymper on the types of female walk), his puns ('equal pay for equal shirk'), the aphorisms ('soup is the best substitute for food I know') which were probably not his own, the violence of his socialist-fascist political views. He felt he had been made a fool of by Whymper and had succumbed to the man's professional charm. In these moods he was unwilling to concede honesty to any of Whymper's actions. He saw only that his own folly and softness were complementary to Whymper's cleverness and ruthlessness.

Of all this he told Margaret nothing. She and Whymper had become great friends. For Whymper's benefit Margaret had extended her party manner: she dropped daring words and was 'unshockable'. She gauged Whymper well. They enjoyed one another's jokes, and each rejoiced that to the other he was a 'character'.

Nor could Mr Stone tell Margaret of his irritation, annoyance, and in some moments his anguish, to find, as he thought, that Whymper was 'riding to success on his back'. These were the words that came to his mind, and they created a picture of almost biblical pitifulness: a lusty, fat-cheeked young man on the back of someone very old, very thin, in rags, supporting his feebleness on a staff. Mr Stone could no longer hide from himself his displeasure at finding their names, Whymper and Stone, coupled so frequently. Always in such items in the house magazine it was Whymper who was quoted, so that over the months it had begun to appear that Whymper was the Unit. His own contribution, his passion and anguish had gone for nothing, had gone to magnify Whymper. Out of his life had come this one idea; for this single creation his life had been changed for good, perhaps destroyed. And it had gone to magnify Whymper, young Whymper, whose boast was that he made nothing.

Yet with this there remained the concern for Whymper that had grown out of their relationship, a concern that was almost parental and at times was like pity. Between what Whymper saw himself to be and what he was the gap was too great. His attempts at smartness were pathetic. His clothes were good; he wore them badly. He tapped his cigarette with such careful elegance; when the cigarette came out from between his bruised lips it was wet and disagreeable to see. Attempting authority, he frequently only invited rebuff; and though he seemed always half to expect rebuff, he had never learned to handle it. And like a reproach to Mr Stone was Whymper's growing and often proclaimed affection for Margaret and himself, an affection for which, in spite of everything, Mr Stone found that he was grateful and pleased, and perhaps a little surprised, for in the office their relationship continued to be formal.

About himself Whymper spoke continually, but about his family he had little to say. He was a Londoner. His father still lived in Barnet, but when Whymper spoke of him it was as of someone far away and unimportant. His mother he never mentioned. He was a man without a family, someone who belonged only to the city. As secret as his parents he kept his house. He seldom spoke of it except to indicate that it was fully owned by him. All his important activities appeared to take place outside it, and Margaret and Mr Stone began to feel that his house was not a place to which Whymper invited anyone. They were both surprised, then, when one evening after dinner he said, 'I just can't keep on eating this muck of Margaret's. You must come and have dinner with me, just to see what can be done with food.'

His house was in Kilburn, on that side of the High Road which gave him a Hampstead telephone number. It was an undistinguished terrace house with no garden. Whymper lived on the ground floor; the basement and other floors he rented out. Margaret and Mr Stone sat in the front room while Whymper busied himself in the kitchen, which was at the end of the hallway, on the landing of the basement stairs. The front room was roughly and sparsely furnished. There was a type of buff-coloured matting on the floor. The two armchairs were perfunctorily modern, their simplicity already turned to shabbiness. A bullfighting poster, dusty at the top, was fixed with yellowing adhesive tape to one wall; the other walls were bare. The bookcase was a jumble of paperbacks, old newspapers and copies of *Esquire, Time* and the *Spectator*; separate from this was a neat shelf of green Penguins. To Margaret and Mr Stone, who had expected something grander, something more in keeping with Whymper's clothes, the room spoke of loneliness. While they sat waiting, they heard footsteps in the hall and on the stairs: Whymper's tenants.

He brought in the food plate by plate. His plates and dishes had been chosen with greater care than his furniture. The first thing he offered was a plateful of cold sliced beef below a thick layer of finely chipped lettuce, cabbage, carrots, capsicums and garlic, all raw. Then he brought out a tall, slender bottle.

'Olive oil,' he said.

Margaret let a few drops fall onto her plate.

'It isn't going to explode,' he said, taking the bottle away from her. 'Like this.' He poured with a slow, circular motion. 'Go on. Eat it up.' He did the same for Mr Stone, then went out to the kitchen.

Margaret and Mr Stone sat silently in the dim light, staring at the plates on their napkined knees.

'You remember during the war,' Whymper said, coming back, 'how those starving Poles didn't have nice white bread like ours and were living on *black* bread? It's just ten times as good as our cotton wool, that's all. Don't have a *slice*, Margaret. Break off a hunk. None of your fish-and-chips graces tonight, dear. Have some butter with it. You too, Stone.'

They broke off hunks.

He left them again.

'What are we going to do, Doggie?'

He returned with a label-less bottle of yellow fluid.

'Don't wait for me,' he said. He filled three tumblers. 'This used to be a great wine-drinking country. Today you people with your one bottle of Beaujolais think it's something you sip. What do you think of that, Stone? It's the resin that gives it the flavour.'

He sat opposite them. 'Mm!' he said, sniffing at his plate with mock disgust. 'Those dirty foreigners, eating all this garlic and grease. Where's the tomato ketchup?' He started champing through his chipped grass and olive oil, drinking retsina, biting at his hunk of black bread, and maintained a steady flow of cheerful talk, mainly about food, while they nibbled and sipped.

Afterwards they had biscuits with brie and camembert. And then he gave them turkish coffee out of a long-handled, shining copper jug.

They returned home extremely hungry, but feeling extraordinarily affectionate towards the ridiculous young man. A day or two later they were agreeing that the dinner was 'just like Whymper'.

And it was as though, having invited Mr Stone to his home, he had decided that there was no longer to be any reserve between them. Now they often had lunch together, Whymper initiating Mr Stone into the joys of travelling about London by taxi in the middle of the day at Excal's expense. And Mr Stone was subjected to Whymper's confessions.

It turned out in the first place that Whymper had a 'mistress'. He used the word with a tremendous casualness. She was a radio actress whose name Mr Stone knew only vaguely but which for Whymper's sake he pretended to know very well. Whymper spoke of her as a public figure, and was full of stories of her sexual rapacity. It appeared that food had a disturbing effect on her. Once, according to Whymper, when they were in a restaurant she had suddenly abandoned her main course, picked up her bag and said, 'Pay the bill and let's go home and –'

'She tears the clothes off you,' Whymper added.

Mr Stone regretted encouraging Whymper, for Whymper's talk became increasingly of sex. The details he gave of his actress mistress were intimate and embarrassing. And once, after a dinner at the Stones', he said of Gwen, 'I feel that if I squeeze that girl she will ooze all sorts of sexual juices.'

Overwhelmed by the word 'mistress' and by Whymper's talk, Mr Stone was beginning to doubt that the actress existed, when Whymper arranged a meeting one lunchtime in a pub. ('Daren't give her lunch,' Whymper said.) She was, disappointingly, over thirty, with a face that was over-powdered, lips that were carelessly painted, and teary eyes. She gave an impression of length: her face was thin and long, she had no bust to speak of, and her bottom, long rather than broad, hung very low. There was nothing of the actress, as Mr Stone had imagined the type, about her, either in looks or voice. He could not imagine her tearing the clothes off anyone, but he was glad that she was sufficiently excited by Whymper to wish to tear off his clothes; and he was glad that Whymper was sufficiently excited by her to permit this. Towards them both he felt paternal: he thought they were lucky to find one another.

'She's a very charming person,' he said afterwards.

And Whymper said: 'I can put my head between her legs and stay there for hours.'

He spoke with an earnestness that was like sadness. And

thereafter the sight of Whymper rolling a cigarette between his lips always brought back this unexpected, frightening, joyless sentence.

After this meeting, Mr Stone heard nothing of the actress for some time. Instead Whymper let drop talk, disconnected and vague, as though the humiliations were still close, of his childhood and army experiences. 'We were listening to the Coronation on the wireless, with some of my mother's friends. And I was quite big, you know. My mother said, "Come and look, Bill. They're coming down the street." And I went and looked. I went. They all roared with laughter. I could have killed her.' 'They say the army makes a man. It nearly broke me. You know the old British soldier. "Terribly" stupid and "frightfully" brave. I was neither.'

Sometimes he kept up a running commentary of contempt on everything he saw. This could be amusing. Once, just as they turned into a street, he said, 'Look at that idiot.' And before them, as though conjured up by Whymper's words, was a man in bloated motor-cyclist's garb, the low-hanging seat of which was stained with monkey-like markings. There were days when the sight of black men on the London streets drove him to fury; he spent the whole of one lunchtime walk loudly counting those he saw, until both he and Mr Stone burst out laughing. But these midday walks with Whymper also had their embarrassments. Well-dressed women with their daughters infuriated him as much as black men; and once, when they were behind such a couple on a traffic island at Oxford Circus, Mr Stone heard him mutter, 'Get out of the way, you old bitch.' He frequently muttered abuse like this in crowds. But this time he had spoken too loudly. The woman turned, gave him a slow look of deep contempt, at which he seemed to cringe; and the depression that came upon him persisted until they returned to the office.

He was going through a difficult time. He appeared to cling to Mr Stone. One day, when they were having lunch, Whymper said with sudden passion, 'I wish I were like you, Stone. I wish my life was over. I wish everything had already happened.'

'How do you know my life is over?'

'I can't bear the thought of having to go on. It must be so nice to look back, to be what one is. To have done it all, to know that one had done it all. To be calm, blissfully calm, day after day, having tea on a fresh clean tablecloth on a green lawn.'

His words pierced Mr Stone, rousing him out of his concern for Whymper, recalling a past that was so near and now so inaccessible. How right Whymper was, and how wrong! And these words of Whymper's, which he thought almost poetic, remained with him like the words of a song, with the power always to move.

Day by day, then, Whymper's confidences became disquieting.

'I am a changed man,' he said one lunchtime. 'As from today. How can I *signalize* this change, Stone?'

'I can't really think.'

'A hat, Stone. A man needs a hat. A hat makes a man. Look at you. Look at the people wearing hats. Where can I buy one?'

'I buy mine at Dunn's. There's a branch at the end of Oxford Street.'

'Good. We'll go to Dunn's.'

They hustled through the lunchtime crowd, Whymper chanting, 'A hat, a hat. Must get a hat.'

And when they got to the Dunn's window Whymper stopped dead and gaped, his determination abruptly gone, his new character abandoned.

'I didn't know,' he said softly, 'that hats were so expensive.'

For some time they stood, their back to the window, studying the crowded street, until Mr Stone said they had better be getting on.

Whymper had not been looking well, his eyes sunken, his face sallow; and one morning he came into the office looking ravaged and ill.

'I was in her garden all night,' he said to Mr Stone at lunch.

This was the first reference to his mistress since the meeting in the pub.

'I saw them have dinner' – remembering the effect of food on Whymper's mistress, Mr Stone prepared to smile, but Whymper was telling it as no joke – 'and I watched until they drew the curtains. Then I stayed until he left. I couldn't leave. It was hell.'

'Who was this other – chap?'

Whymper gave the name of a minor and declining television personality, speaking it with the casualness he used for the word 'mistress'.

Mr Stone permitted himself to be impressed. But Whymper's pride had already vanished in his distress, and Mr Stone very much wanted to comfort him.

'I should think,' he said, 'that that settles that. She sounds a most unreliable person, and if I were you I shouldn't see her again.'

'Very well!' Whymper said angrily. 'I will see that you don't meet her again. Ever.'

And that was the end not only of Whymper's stories about his mistress, but also of his confidences and their lunchtime outings. With Mr Stone in the office Whymper was again the efficient hard man of action, and there was nothing in his manner to indicate that he had once damagingly revealed himself to Mr Stone.

The crisis or crises in Whymper's personal life in no way affected his work for the Knights Companion. His mind continued as restless and inventive as ever. He established a competition for Knights Companion. It was difficult to work out a basis for awarding points and in the end they decided that the prize should go to someone of his and Mr Stone's choice. *Oyez! Oyez!* continued to encourage the belief that a carefully marked competition was afoot, and late in November announced that the prize was to be presented by Sir Harry at a Christmas Round Table dinner.

This dinner greatly exercised and stimulated Whymper, and he had continually to be restrained by Mr Stone. His first idea was that the Knights Companion should appear in antique costume of some sort. When this was rejected he suggested that the toastmaster should wear chainmail, real or imitation, that the waiters should wear Elizabethan dress (Whymper's feeling for period was romantic and inexact), and that there should be musicians, also in Elizabethan dress, playing Elizabethan music.

'The music would be just right,' he said. 'You know it? Tinkle, tinkle, scrape and tinkle. The old boys being bowed to their seats. Tinkle, tinkle. We could hire the costumes from the Old Vic.'

Mr Stone said he didn't think any self-respecting restaurant or waiter would care for that.

'Hire costumes from the Old Vic?' Whymper said, growing light-headed. 'We'll hire the Old Vic.'

Calmer, he pleaded for the toastmaster in chainmail, then for a doorman in armour, and finally for a suit of armour in the doorway. He settled for archaically worded invitations in gothic lettering on parchment-like paper.

On the night nearly all of those who had promised to attend turned up, many bearing their scroll-like invitations. Among the earliest was the former department head of whom nothing had been heard since his acknowledgement of the cheque for £249 17s 5½d. He entered with the appearance of someone deeply offended. But his name aroused no recognition in Whymper or Mr Stone, who, though passingly puzzled by his frown and two-finger handshake, were more interested in his companion. It seemed that a fresh humiliation awaited the former department head, for contrary to the explicit men-only instructions of the invitation and the Round Table publicity, he had brought his wife, who was even now, having shaken hands with Whymper and Mr Stone, penetrating deeper into the chamber where elderly men, variously dressed in lounge suits and dinner jackets, were standing in subdued, embarrassed groups.

Whymper acted quickly.

'Ladies in the bower,' he said, catching up with her and blocking her progress.

A few words to the head-waiter had their effect. The lady was led, surprised but unprotesting, to another room on the same floor, where for some little time she sat in solitude.

Whymper's action proved a blessing. For a number of Knights Companion ('What can you do with the bastards?' Whymper muttered) brought their ladies, and the bower gradually filled.

Sir Harry arrived. His presence gave depth and meaning to the silence. Such a small man, though, to be so important!

Names were looked for on charts, places found and the dinner began. Now and again camera bulbs flashed and the diners blinked. The Press was represented in force and their effect on the waiters was profound.

The meal over, the Queen toasted ('God bless her,' Whymper said with a straight face), it was time for Sir Harry to make his speech. He pulled out some typewritten sheets from his breast pocket and the room was hushed. It was known that he prepared his speeches carefully, writing down every word, and it was an article of faith in Excal that his English could not be bettered.

They were meeting, Sir Harry said, to celebrate their fellowship and to do honour to one of their number. That they had gathered together to do this had, however, a deeper significance. He thought it proved three things. It proved in the first place that Excal did not consider its obligations to an employee ended when the employee's own responsibilities were over. In the second place it proved that in Excal it was possible for anyone with drive and determination to rise, regardless of his age. Mr Stone was an example of this. (At this there was applause and Mr Stone didn't know where to look.) It also proved that teamwork was of the essence in an organization like Excal. That the Unit was a success could not be denied. That it had been successful was due to the effort and faith of three persons. If congratulations were in order, and he thought they were, then congratulations, like Gaul, ought to be divided into three parts. Congratulations to Mr Stone. Congratulations to Mr Whymper.

'And last – aha!' He looked up roguishly from his typewritten script. 'You thought I was going to say "and last but not least"! And last and *also* least, the person who intends to keep you no longer from the main business and true star of the evening.'

He sat down amid frenzied applause, a little wiping of rheumy eyes, and cries of 'Good old Harry!' from those whom the occasion roused to a feeling of fellowship greater than they had known during their service. As soon as he sat down he looked preoccupied and indifferent to the applause and busied himself with a grave conversation with the man beside him.

Whymper was the next speaker. He spoke of the competition and of the difficulty they had had in coming to a decision. One man would get the prize, but the prize was in a way for all of them, since they were meeting, as Sir Harry had so rightly stressed, to celebrate their fellowship.

And the climax came.

'Silence! Silence!' the toastmaster called.

There was silence.

'Let Jonathan Richard Dawson, Knight Companion, rise and advance!'

(The ritual and words had been devised by Whymper.)

From one end of the horse-shoe table an old man in a tweed suit arose, bespectacled, vaguely chewing and looking rather wretched. Followed by hundreds of watery eyes, and in absolute silence, he advanced right up to the centre to Sir Harry, who, standing once more, took a sword from an attendant and presented it. A score of camera bulbs flashed, and in the newspapers the next morning the scene appeared: the presentation of the sword *Excal*ibur to the Knight Companion of the year.

It was a week of Christmas lunches and dinners and staff parties, and on the next evening Mr Stone and Margaret had to go to the Tomlinsons'. To this Mr Stone looked forward with greater pleasure than he had to the Round Table dinner. For he was going as a private person among friends who had not that day had the advantage of seeing their names, and a photograph in which they were clearly visible, in the newspapers; and he was going as someone who was not at all puffed up by such publicity but was taking it calmly, someone who still among his friends could be natural and unspoilt.

Mr Stone could tell, from the welcome they received at the door and from Tony Tomlinson's lingering attentions, that he and Margaret were the stars of the party. The photograph was not mentioned, and it was with an indescribable pleasure that he led the conversation to perfectly normal and even commonplace subjects. His gestures became slower and more relaxed. He studied himself, and the word that came to him was 'urbane'. He was perceptibly fussy and longwinded in deciding between sweet and dry sherry, as one who felt that his decision was of importance and was being watched by many. Still, he felt, with the steady erosion of the main course and the imminent approach of the dessert, that the determination of Tomlinson and Tomlinson's guests to maintain a silence on the issue which he felt was consuming them was a little excessive. He even slightly withdrew from the commonplace talk in which he had earlier so actively participated. And it was with relief that he heard Grace say, 'It's so nice for Richard and Margaret, don't you think?'

There was an instant chorus of undemonstrative approval.

'You wouldn't believe it,' Grace went on. 'But they met under this very roof just two years ago.'

'. . . just two years ago,' Tomlinson echoed.

Margaret at once took over.

'For the last six months I've been hearing about nothing else,' she said. 'If I hear another word about those doddering old men of Richard's I believe I'll scream.'

'Well, of course, it's your own fault, Margaret,' Grace

said. 'We've been telling Richard for years that every man needs a woman behind him.'

'How unsatisfactory!' Margaret said, rocking in her seat, as she did after delivering a witticism.

Mr Stone recognized the influence of Whymper and covertly examined the table for reactions. But there was only pleasure. Even the demure, unspeaking wife of the unspeaking chief accountant, though red to the tips of her ears, was smiling at her plate. At this dinner, it was clear, Margaret could set the tone and dictate her own terms.

And if he needed further proof of their position of command that evening, it came when the ladies had been led away, and the men, standing drinkless and cigarless, with funny hats on their heads, prepared to make conversation. Now all the delight he had bottled up throughout the evening overflowed. His funny hat pushed to the back of his head, his face a constant smile, absently taking the nuts which Tomlinson gravely pressed on him, he led the talk. And now it was his words that Tomlinson listened to, it was his words that Tomlinson echoed.

'It's like a religious movement,' he said, rising on his toes, making a lifting gesture with both arms and throwing a handful of nuts into his mouth.

'... yes, a religious movement,' Tomlinson said, with the pained expression with which he always uttered his echoes.

'Why not get our old boys to visit the old boys of clients, they said. But' – wagging a nut-filled hand and chewing – '"Why?" I said. "This is not to help Excal. This is to help all those poor old people without friends, without relations, without – without *any*thing."' He threw more nuts into his mouth.

'... of course, helping the poor old people ...'

'Of course,' said the chief accountant, speaking through a mouthful of half-chewed nut and swallowing hurriedly when his words issued blurred, 'an idea is one thing, but the packaging is another. And that's where I hand it to you. Packaging. Everybody's interested in packaging these days.'

'Packaging, of course,' Mr Stone said, momentarily faltering before delight again swept him on. 'We had to get the old boys out on the road and up to the various front doors.'

'... yes, packaging ...'

But before Mr Stone could modify his views on packaging Tomlinson said they ought to be joining the ladies.

And to the ladies Margaret was saying, 'Well, that's what I tell Richard when he gets depressed.' (When was he depressed?) 'It's so much better to have success now than to have a flash in the pan at thirty.'

Dear Doggie! When did they ever discuss the point? When did she ever say such words to him?

It was an evening of pure delight. He would look back and see that it marked the climax of his life.

6

For as soon as the door closed behind them and they were alone in the empty lamplit street, he no longer wished to talk. He wished only to savour the unusual mood. Margaret, sensing the change in him, was silent. And as the minutes passed, steadily separating him from the brilliance, it was as though the brilliance was something already lost, a hallucination that could never be captured again; and his silence developed into a type of irritability, which might never have found expression had not Margaret, no longer able to keep herself in, begun to talk, party platitudes, party comments, while they were in the taxi. By that shrug of his shoulders with which he expressed his distaste for her, his wish to be alone and separate from her, he forced her to silence, and in silence they returned home. So, unexpectedly, the evening ended.

And the further the brilliance receded the more clearly he recognized its unusual quality. It was a brilliance which was incapable of being sustained, yet a brilliance of which every diminution was a loss to be mourned, a reminder of darkness that had been lived through and a threat of the darkness that was to come.

It was again that difficult time of year when with Christmas and the New Year the workaday world was in abeyance, the season of rest and goodwill which throws everyone more deeply into himself and makes the short days long. The holiday was not at all what they had planned. His mood did not lift. The brilliance he sought to repossess grew more shadowy; and with helpless rage, both rage and helplessness stimulated by the absence of the people against whom he raged, his mind returned again and again to certain things which during his brilliance he had ignored but which now could not be denied. There was Sir Harry's speech. There was Whymper. There was the chief accountant's knowing little remark about packaging, doubtless picked up from some magazine or newspaper. Other people had made his idea their property, and they were riding on his back. They had taken the one idea of an old man, ignoring the pain out of which it was born, and now he was no longer necessary to them. Even if he were to die, the Whympers and Sir Harrys would continue to present *Excal*iburs. He would be forgotten together with his pain: a little note in the house magazine, then nothing more.

So impotently during these festive days he raged, and could tell Margaret nothing of what he felt. He feared to make himself ridiculous, and he feared Margaret's impatience: he was sure that she would take the other side and make out quite a case for the Whympers and Sir Harrys. So at last the brilliance dimmed, and all that remained was this anxiety, anger and sense of loss. Any reference to his success reminded him of his present emptiness. 'It has nothing to do with me at all,' he said, the modesty, thought proper, concealing a bitterness that was already turning to sorrow.

And then late one evening, less than a week after the Tomlinsons' party, the telephone rang, shattering the silence. Margaret took off her spectacles and went out to answer it. Her words, few and widely separated, came to him muffled.

When the door opened and Margaret reappeared, he knew.

'That was Grace. Tony's dead.'

He put his pipe down slowly, hearing the slight tap as it touched the table.

'He was watching television at half past eight. At nine o'clock he was dead.'

Tony! So whole, so complete, so Tony-like, so live in the often recollected incidents of that evening!

Margaret came to the back of his chair and put her arms

around his neck, her cheek on his head. It was a theatrical gesture. He appreciated it. But it did not console him.

He went to his study. It was very cold. He turned on the electric fire, sat down and watched its ever-brightening glow, saw the dust on the electric bars make its tiny flares and smelled its burning.

Downstairs Margaret was telephoning.

'He was watching television at half past eight. At nine o'clock he was dead.'

The new year did not bring Mr Stone the reassurance he had been half expecting. There was nothing new to excite or absorb him, and much of the work he was called upon to do was simple routine. So, barring the discussions with Whymper about the Round Table dinner, it had been for many weeks past; but now, with his new eyes, he thought he saw his own position more clearly. He was in the office what he had been in the library, a gentle, endearing man nearing retirement, of no particular consequence. Now he saw how often in a crisis the instinct of the 'staff' was to turn to Whymper, for Whymper's quick thinking, his ability to see his way out of a jam, was legendary – 'ladies in the bower' had already become an office story – and though not liked, he was respected. He saw that he was entrusted with what might be considered safe: the supervision of lists, the overlooking of accounts. He had declined into 'staff' himself. To this assumption there was nothing with which he could reply. He did not have Whymper's restless mind; he had no new idea to offer; he was unable to handle the public relations – and this aspect of the Unit's work had grown more important since the publicity – with Whymper's skill. He became snappish in the office; he became rude. And there occurred a row with Whymper over a typist of Polish origin.

Enraged by her inadequate grammar, sloppy dress and what he thought was her insolence, he had quarrelled with her in public and gone so far as to refer to her as 'that D.P. girl'. He was in his office scourging himself for his behaviour when Whymper entered in a tremendous temper, his eyes narrow, his lips quivering, Whymper of all people, the man who during those lunchtime walks had spoken with so much feeling about 'foreigners cluttering up the place'. His performance was melodramatic and self-appraising from start to finish, from 'What's this I hear, Stone?' to 'Don't you dare talk to any of the staff like that again, do you hear?' Mr Stone saw through it all but was none the less cowed. It occurred to him that the girl might be Whymper's new mistress, and several replies to Whymper's threat came into his head. But he had the lucidity to remain silent.

He thought, however, to revenge himself on them the following day. The girl had typed 'artillery' for 'itinerary' in a letter to a distinguished Knight Companion. He did not point out the error to her. Instead, he put an asterisk after the word and wrote a footnote: 'I leave this in because I feel that this example of our typists' literacy will amuse you. The word should, of course, be "itinery".' It was a heavy joke, made at the end of the day; perhaps the judgement of early morning might have shown him as much. Two days later the reply came: 'It seems that typists' literacy is catching. By "itinery" I imagine you mean "itinerary".' Now he knew very well how the word ought to be spelt; and in this swift rebuke he saw some sort of judgement, which made him desist from his war against the girl and made him less anxious to impose himself in the office.

His relationship with Whymper underwent a further change. Whymper's attitude was now one of strict formality, and in view of their respective power in the office this formality was like indifference. The quarrel over the typist was scarcely the reason. It seemed, rather, that in the days since the Round Table dinner Whymper had progressively lost interest in the Knights Companion, and having lost interest in them, had lost interest in Mr Stone as well. And this to Mr Stone was additionally galling, that though Whymper's interest in the Unit had declined, his power and fame as its representative steadily increased.

From the office, then, once the source of so much excitement, the source of his new vigour, he turned once more to his home. Here everything spoke of the status which he could not fully feel in the office: the re-decorated rooms, the organization of his household, Miss Millington's banging of the dinner gong (a process that ever lengthened), Margaret's dinner parties.

At these parties, to which Whymper continued to come, though less often than before, there was now a new fixture: Grace. Margaret was performing with zest for her what she had once performed for Margaret. And Grace was as radiant a widow as Margaret had been. From the first wan, teary-eyed appearance, with a brave sad smile, the gaunt creature had in spite of fogs and wintry drizzles visibly blossomed from week to week. The gradual attenuation which, as though to approximate to the appearance of her husband, she had been undergoing was abruptly arrested. The lined, thin face filled out; the neck lost some of its scragginess; the eyes brightened; the voice, always deep, grew deeper and more positive. Even in her movements there was freedom, as though some restraint had been removed. Whereas before she had been content to sit vaguely round-shouldered and apparently enervated in a chair, drawling out comments, often her husband's, with an occasional baring of very white false teeth, now there was a liveliness, a pertness, an independence. Her hairstyle changed. And, at first noticed by Margaret alone, who did not think it fair to Grace to mention it or to betray her to Mr Stone, new clothes and new ornaments began appearing on the aged creature. This taste, once released, became an obsession. Margaret continued only to observe until, no longer able to bear the silence, Grace spoke. And it was at a display of recent acquisitions that Mr Stone surprised them one Sunday afternoon in a childish huddle, those two women who, meeting at the door, had been so world-weary, one brave, the other grave.

Then for ten whole days there was no visit from Grace. When she reappeared she looked fit but saddened. She had been, she said, to Paris; and she suggested that her action was partly the result of her distracted state. She was walking down Bond Street in the middle of the day and had seen the Air France building. Yielding to impulse, she had gone in and inquired whether there was a seat on any of the Paris planes that day, behaving as though the matter was one of urgency; had booked and paid; had raced home in a taxi to get passport, had raced in the taxi to the bank to get traveller's cheques, and then, with minutes to spare, had made the West Kensington air terminal for the airport bus. Throughout she had had no control of herself and had acted as one crazed. The trip, not surprisingly, had given her little pleasure. But for Margaret she had a gift: a bottle of 'Robe d'un Soir' perfume by Carven (one of a set of three bottles bought on the BEA plane back). She had bought a number of other things as well: she had in her haste forgotten to pack all the clothes she needed. Some of the things she was wearing; a number of the smaller items she had brought with her; and Margaret, with an approval that diminished as the display lengthened, made approving comments.

This was the first of Grace's disappearances. When in the middle of March she returned tanned, with cheeks almost full, from Majorca, she said to Mr Stone, 'You have to do *some*thing, haven't you?'

At last even Margaret's loyalty, in spite of Grace's gifts, was strained. Mr Stone's stupefaction turned to downright disapproval. But nothing could be said, for with each succeeding escapade Grace showed herself more anxious for their support.

Tony was never mentioned. At first this had been due to delicacy. Later it seemed that, as a result of Grace's strenuous efforts to forget, he had indeed been forgotten.

And sometimes it occurred to Mr Stone that he was surrounded by women – Margaret, Grace, Olive, Gwen, Miss Millington – and that these women all lived in a world of dead or absent men.

Winter still ruled, but there was the promise of spring in

the morning sunshine which each day grew less thin. Slanting through the black branches of the tree it fell, the palest gilding, on the decaying grey-black roof of the outhouse next door. And there one morning Mr Stone saw his old enemy, the black cat. It was asleep. Even as Mr Stone watched, the cat woke, stretched itself in a slow, luxurious, assured action, and rose. It was as if the world was awakening from winter. Then, leisurely, still drowsy from its sleep in the sunshine, the cat made its way along the length of board which the man next door had attached from outhouse to fence (perhaps to keep the fence from complete collapse, or the outhouse, or to support each to the other). Along the top of the broken fence the cat walked to the back, and leapt lightly down into the grounds of the girls' school. Idly, frequently pausing to look, it paced about the damp grass until, bored, it returned to its own ruinous garden and licked itself. It looked up and Mr Stone was confronted with the eyes that had stared at him two years before from the top of his dark steps. He tapped on the window. The cat turned, walked to its back fence and settled itself in a gap, sticking its head out into the school grounds, revealing only the caricature of a cat's back to Mr Stone.

For Mr Stone this appearance of the cat marked the end of winter, and morning after morning he watched the cat stretch and rise and make its aimless perambulation about its garden and the school grounds. His hostility to the animal had long ago died, living only in the almost forgotten story of Margaret's. And now he was taken not only by the animal's idle elegance, but also by its loneliness. He came to feel that the cat watched for him every morning just as he watched for it. One morning when he tapped on the window the cat did not turn and walk away. So he tapped on the window every morning, and the cat unfailingly responded, looking up with blank patient eyes. He played games with it, tapping on the window, crouching behind the wall, then standing up again. 'You're behaving like an old fool,' he sometimes thought. And indeed one day when he had been knocking and making noises through the glass at the cat, he heard Margaret say, 'What's the matter, Doggie? You'll be late if you don't hurry up.'

One of her recent complaints was that he was taking longer and longer to do simple things, and the slowness of his gestures was degenerating into absent-mindedness.

His communion with the cat, stretching every morning in the warming sunshine, made him more attentive to the marks of the approaching spring. It extended his observations from the tree in the school grounds to every tree and shrub he saw on the way to work. He took an interest in the weather columns of the newspapers, studying the temperatures, the times of the rising and setting of the sun, noting how, though the days seemed equally short, the afternoons frequently dissolving in rain and fog, the newspapers each day announced a lengthening of daylight. He noticed the approaching spring in the behaviour of people on the streets and in the train, in the advertisements in the newspapers and even in the letters to the editor. One letter in particular he remembered, from the chatty letter column of a popular newspaper he sometimes read in the office. It was by a girl who had taken care to indicate her age, which was sixteen, in brackets after her name. She protested sternly at the behaviour of men in springtime. Men, she wrote, stared so 'hungrily'. 'Sometimes,' she ended fiercely, 'I feel I would really like to give them an eyeful.' It was such a joyous letter. It spoke with such innocent assurance of the coming of spring.

He observed. But participation was denied him. It was like his 'success', from which at its height he had felt cut off, and which reminded him only of his emptiness and the darkness to come. A new confirmation of his futility presently arrived. For reasons which in his own mind were confused – his restlessness, his fear of imprisonment at home, his hope that given more time he might do something that would be his very own, something that would truly release him – he had been making vague inquiries about the possible deferment of his retirement, which was to take place that July. He had been met, as it seemed he had always been met, with a gentle humouring, a statement that he had done enough, and a joke that there would be no trouble about his appointment as a Knight Companion and that he stood a good chance of getting *Excal*ibur next year.

He did not relish the joke. It deepened his distaste for the work he did day by day; deepened his distaste for Whymper, now curiously withdrawn and adding an abruptness to his formality, all of which Mr Stone thought he saw through but which nevertheless annoyed him; it deepened his sense of loss, and made him hug more closely the anxiety and anger which was all that remained of that evening of brilliance.

Beyond spring lay summer and retirement and those days of which Whymper had spoken: 'To be calm, blissfully calm, day after day, having tea on a fresh clean tablecloth on a green lawn.'

For these days Margaret was already preparing. She spoke of the need for activity: idleness was to be kept at bay. She was already planning visits and tours, and Grace, whose helpfulness suggested that she might not be unwilling to accompany them, was full of advice. It was clear, however, that one preliminary was unavoidable. Miss Millington would have to go. The old woman had aged and thickened considerably during the last few months, possibly because of the labours that had been imposed on her and which she had willingly undertaken. Though she had not lost any of her enthusiasm and did her best to conceal the failing of her flesh, not even the smartest uniform could now hide the fact that she had ceased to be an ornament and had declined far beyond the stage of the old retainer occasionally called in to help. Her shuffle had become a painful crawl, and it could not be denied that she smelled. She was often found dozing in the kitchen where she had once made her inimitable chips. One day she dropped the dinner gong on her foot. The gong was dented, and for this she was dreadfully sorry. Her own pain she concealed, but her foot swelled, and remained swollen; the flesh, progressively failing, could only yield. Once she slopped some soup over the jacket of a high official from Welfare, and in a feeble reflex of concern had poured the remainder into his lap.

And once she nearly killed Margaret. The brass bell had been rung to summon her. And presently, shuffling out of the Master's study, Miss Millington appeared at the top of the stair well with the bread knife in her hand. What was she doing up there with the bread knife? But so it was now with the aged soul: she had some minutes before been making sandwiches in the kitchen downstairs for the Master's tea. She appeared, then, holding the bread knife. And even as Margaret looked up the bread knife slipped out of Miss Millington's grasp and, steadied by the weight of its bone handle, plummeted dagger-like down, not more than two inches from Margaret's head, and stuck upright and quivering, as though thrown by an expert knife-thrower, into the telephone table. Margaret had stood transfixed, had refused to touch the knife, which had sunk in quite deep. And by the time Miss Millington had descended the stairs, step by step, at every step uttering garbled apologies in her gasping voice, the door bell had rung, Mr Stone had been admitted by a shaken Margaret, and there, next to the telephone, like the emblem of a secret society, the bread knife stood before him.

So Miss Millington had to go. But before she went there were discussions, which enabled Margaret to taste power and even sweeter compassion. Whereas before the two women had entered into conspiracies to keep disagreeable things from the Master, now Margaret attempted to engage Mr Stone in conspiratorial discussions about Miss Millington. But he was not interested; he appeared reluctant to come to a decision. So Margaret turned to Grace. And often, in whispers, when Miss Millington was out of the room, the old servant's failings were talked over, and it was agreed that firmness was as much in order as compassion. When Miss Millington entered the room there was silence.

For a moment the women stared at the creature's pallid, puffy baby-face, her netted hair below her scarf, her long skirts. Then Margaret would speak to her in a voice that was just too loud, as one might do when requiring an animal to perform its tricks. And the decrepit creature, like an animal scenting the slaughterhouse, would make hurried, gasping and unintelligible talk, still anxious to prove her activity and usefulness, appealing, it seemed, not to Margaret but to Grace, whose full tanned face remained as seeming-smiling and full of teeth as always.

There came a day when Margaret was out of the house – she had gone to a sale with Grace, such shopping occasions having become more important to them both – and Mr Stone was alone at home with Miss Millington. He announced that he was going up to the study. He did nothing there which he could not have done more easily in the office, but he preferred now to bring some of his work home, as though hoping to find again in the study the passion and vigour which had once driven him night after night, working in the warm pool of light at the desk that had come to the house with Margaret.

It was while he was there that he heard a voice booming up indistinctly through the house. He called: 'Miss Millington!' But the booming did not abate. He opened the door and went out to the landing.

It was Miss Millington. He saw her below him in the hall, sitting in the chair next to the telephone table, talking into the telephone in a voice which held conspiracy and which she must have felt to be a whisper, but which was a breathless shouting that echoed and re-echoed in the hall and up the stairs. She was wearing her white apron. Her head scarf was on the table, and he could see the net on her grey hair.

'She thinks I tried to kill her,' she was saying. 'With the bread knife. She doesn't say so. But I know that's what's on her mind. It will be stealing next. Though there's precious little of hers to steal. I believe she's gone mad. The Master? He's gone very strange. To tell the truth, I don't know what's happening to the place. I don't see how I can stay on here, not with all that's going on.'

To whom was she speaking? Who, in all the huge city, was the person to whom Miss Millington could turn for comfort, to whom she was speaking with such security, such an assurance of sympathetic reception? Of her life outside the house – her relationship with Eddie and Charley, 'just finishing the fish shop', the children for whom she bought sweets, the nephew in Camden Town she sometimes went to see – he knew very little. And now this saddened him. But more than this was the warmth that started in him for the creature who could scarcely disguise her hurt by her show of dignity, which both he and Margaret had assumed to be dead.

And all he could say was, 'Miss Millington! Miss Millington!'

But she was deafened by her own booming.

It wasn't until he was half way down the stairs, shouting her name ever more loudly as he approached her own thundering, that she looked up, tears drying on her cheeks, less like the marks of emotion than of physical decay, no guilt on her face, no realization of having been caught out.

'Yes, sir,' she said into the telephone. And in the same soft tone, which was like silence, she said, 'I have to ring off now.' Then, as though there was still need for secrecy, she pressed her lips together and put the telephone lightly into its cradle, pressing her lips harder when the telephone bell gave its tinkle.

He said, 'I wonder what's keeping Mrs Stone?'

What could he say?

And Miss Millington, by a reflex action dusting the telephone table with her head scarf, quite ineffectually, said, 'Well, you know how it is with these sales, sir. And Mrs Tomlinson is with her.'

Margaret sometimes talked to Grace about moving to the country after Mr Stone retired. She had no intention of doing so – she never spoke of it to Mr Stone – but she felt that such talk was suitable. It also enabled her to indicate to Grace her helpless awareness that the street was no longer what it was. For some time, in fact, and even before Margaret came to it, the street had been changing. Once the habitation mainly of the old and the settled, it was now being invaded by the married young. More prams were pushed about the street. Houses were being turned into flats. Bright 'To Let' and 'For Sale' notices in red, white and black appeared with growing frequency amid the green of hedges, and were almost fixtures in the gardens of some houses which continually changed hands: petty speculators had moved in. Eddie and Charley – E. Beeching and C. Bryant, Builders and Decorators – cheerful red faces between grey caps and white overalls, popped up regularly in the street, now painting this wall, now mending that roof, now visible through uncurtained windows in some stripped front room. A Jamaican family of ferocious respectability (they received no negro callers, accepted no negro lodgers for the room they let, and they kept a budgerigar) moved into one of the houses, which Eddie and Charley promptly repainted, inside and out: its gleaming black-pointed red brick was like a reproach to the rest of the street.

In this ferment the people next door decided to move. So Margaret reported. The house, she said, was too big for the Midgeleys. She had found out their name, and was quoting Mrs Midgeley, with whom, in spite of the black cat, the rank garden and the ruined fence, she appeared to be on cordial terms. They were moving to a new town, where, Margaret said, sticking up for the street, they would be 'more comfortable'.

To Mr Stone the Midgeleys were still newcomers – he slightly resented learning their name – and he did not realize the importance of Margaret's news until the following morning, when he saw the cat sitting in the gap in the fence, its back expressive of boredom, waiting for those early arrivals among the young girls who, with the warmer weather, now drifted up to this end of the school grounds.

At breakfast he said, 'Well, I imagine we'll soon be seeing the last of that cat.'

'They're having it destroyed,' Margaret said. 'Mrs Midgeley was telling me.'

He went on spooning out his egg.

'The children liked him when he was a kitten. But they don't care for him now. Mrs Midgeley was telling me. My dear' – she seemed to be echoing Mrs Midgeley's tone, which was oddly touched with pride – 'they say he's an absolute terror among the lady-cats of the street.'

His morning play with the cat acquired a new quality. Every morning the animal awakened in sunshine, all its grace intact, all its instincts correct, and all awaiting extinction. He wished to see these instincts exercised, to reassure himself that they had not begun to wither, to wonder at their continuing perfection. He tapped; the cat was instantly alert. He studied its body, followed its sure-footed walk, gazed into its bright eyes. He felt anger and pity. The anger was vague and diffused, only occasionally and by an effort of will focusing on the Midgeleys and their dreadful children. The pity was like love, a desire to rescue and protect and cause to continue. But at the same time there was a great lassitude, an unwillingness to act. And his impulse of love never survived the bathroom.

He observed the cats of the street more closely, seeking the lady-cats among which the black cat had done such damage. Perhaps they were those creatures that sat so sedately on the window-ledges of front rooms, on the tops of fence-posts, on steps, the very creatures that in back gardens became so frivolous and unrestrained, for these animals, as he now saw, had one set of manners for the street and another for back gardens. He sought, too, for possible offspring. One he thought he did see, prowling about in the school grounds, a creature like its sire, black, but furrier and more restless.

Taking over Mrs Midgeley's pride, he saw, at the centre of all the cat activity of the street, his own black cat, which every morning waited for him in attitudes of repose and longing. And gradually, what he had at first thought with such anger and pity – 'You will soon be dead' – became mere words, whose import he had to struggle fully to feel, for they released only a pure sweet emotion of sadness in which the object of his thoughts was forgotten, a short-lived emotion that he sought to stimulate by additional words, which he at first rejected but later came to accept with sad satisfaction: 'You will soon be dead. Like me.' For now the leaves of the spring had hardened and the year would soon be racing to its summer height, and he was left out of this cycle, with which just a year ago he had felt himself so happily in tune.

Thus absorbed, he paid little attention to the preparations of the Midgeleys for departure. There was, indeed, little to see. Shortly after Margaret's announcement the Midgeley's front room had been dismantled and had since shown itself curtainless and bare, with a few desolate-looking sticks of furniture and one stained and tattered mattress. This front room gave the house an abandoned air, as did the front garden, where the non-gardening Midgeleys had a single, untended rose tree that continued dutifully to bear its annual white blooms, pure and startling in their isolated beauty. In this garden there was now always to be seen a collection of cats in the late afternoon. It was as if they had already sensed the neglect of the house and its coming emptiness. They were always on their best front-of-house behaviour, but their number, their silent fellowship in the midst of dereliction, and their seeming vigilance unsettled Mr Stone; and they ignored all his muted attempts to frighten them away.

The uncharacteristic behaviour of one of these cats struck him one afternoon as he came down the street, swinging his new briefcase. The cat, white with brown patches, was restlessly pacing about the garden. Its belly was heavy, and from time to time it did a veritable dance of anguish, throwing itself up in the air. The frenzy of the animal alarmed Mr Stone. He made a threatening gesture, in such a way that an onlooker might have thought he was only changing his briefcase from one hand to another with an unnecessarily large action. The cat's frenzy was stilled; then, surprisingly, it leapt up the fence and fled.

He did not think of this incident again until the following morning, when there was no cat on the outhouse roof, when nothing answered his call, and he knew that the black cat, so whole until the morning before, had been destroyed.

No sweet emotion came to him. He was struck with horror. He was filled with self-disgust and, what he had never expected, fear. Fear made the hair on his arms stand on end. Every familiar gesture of the bathroom ritual became meaningless, a mockery of himself. There was reproach and fear in every reminder of his ability to feel, in the touch of the razor on his chin, the chafing of the towel. He feared to touch or be touched.

'Hurry up, Doggie. You'll miss the news headlines.'

He had been holding the towel in his hands and staring at the mirror.

At breakfast Margaret spoke of her plan. Now that the Midgeleys had gone she intended to break down the collapsing fence before the new people arrived. It wouldn't take much to break it down, and the new people would then be compelled to repair it.

They were in the garden some four weeks later, on a Sunday afternoon. Mr Stone was doing his gardening. Margaret was supervising and encouraging the exercise of this passion, which – men being what they are – had caused a cessation of all other activity in the house. Miss Millington was holding a box of petunia seedlings which Margaret had bought the previous morning, less for Mr Stone's benefit than for that of the very old and despairing man who offered them at the door. Squatting, and advancing with a crab-like motion along the bed, Mr Stone was followed step by step by Miss Millington, who held out the seedling box like a nurse offering instruments to a surgeon. She, poor soul, would not see the flowers that might come: she had not yet been told, but she was leaving in a fortnight. Their conversation while they gardened was mainly about the recent depredations of the young black cat, the offspring of that which had been destroyed. He had, it appeared, inherited the habits of his sire. Miss Millington expressed herself fiercely on the subject, and Margaret looked at her with distant approval and encouragement, in which surprise, amusement and regret were all mingled.

It was a restricted, unnatural conversation, with Miss Millington doing most of the talking. It was made so partly by the presence of Miss Millington herself, and partly by their awareness of the new people next door, whose strangeness had not yet worn off and was still a strain. For Mr Stone the arrival of the new people had at once converted the house next door into enemy territory. From the security of his bathroom window he stared with disapproval at everything that went on. And it was, it seemed, with a similar disapproval of his neighbours that the new owner went frowningly about his tasks. He was short, fat and bald. He smoked a pipe and strutted about his property in his waistcoat with his sleeves rolled up. Mr Stone found him as offensive as his dog, a short, corgi-type mongrel that was as round as a sausage and appeared to sleep all day, his white, excessively washed body dazzling in the sunlight. The animal's reaction to noise was negligently to raise its head, then let it drop down again: the cats remained in possession of the front garden. And as much as Margaret had regretted the unmasculine inactivity of Mr Midgeley, so she now regretted the improving zeal of the new owner. Within days of his arrival Eddie and Charley, traitors, had been called in, and had busied themselves with apparent pleasure about the property. They put up a fence so new, so straight, so well-built, that their own now looked shabby and weathered. The back fence in particular, twisted by the spreading roots of the tree in the school grounds, was almost disgraceful.

So in the back garden, which felt so strange, Mr Stone bedded out his petunias, Miss Millington talked about the black cat, and Margaret occasionally made a whispered comment about the folly of the neighbour in not creosoting his fence. Then in the gathering darkness, still squatting beside the bed, Mr Stone began to speak, negligently. He spoke of the lengthening days. He spoke of the tree in whose shade on hot summer afternoons they would soon be sitting. He spoke of flowers.

The aqueous light deepened to darkness. Lights went on about them, in the neighbour's, and across the school grounds in the Monster's and the Male's.

'Doesn't it make you think, though?' he said. 'Just the other day the tree was so bare. And that dahlia bush. Like dead grass all winter. I mean, don't you think it's just the same with us? That we too will have our spring?'

He stopped. And there was silence. About them outlines blurred, windows brightened. The words he had just spoken lingered in his head. They embarrassed him. The silence of the women embarrassed him. Miss Millington was still holding out the empty box. He stood up, dusted his hands, said he was going to have a wash, and walked through the back door into the dark house.

'Miss Millington,' he heard Margaret say, 'did you hear what the Master's just been saying? What do you think?'

He slackened his step.

He heard Miss Millington begin, 'Well, mum–' and after that the diplomatic old soul only pretended to speak and made a series of gasps which could have stood for anything.

He walked on, was going up the steps. A light came on, feet were wiped on the wire mat, and then there was Margaret saying in her party voice:

'Well, I think it's a lotta rubbish.'

One Sunday twelve years before, when Olive was living in Balham, Mr Stone went to have tea with her and Gwen, who was then just six. He had learned the importance of tea in their lives from an incident that had occurred not long before. They had gone for a walk on Clapham Common. About four Olive said they should be getting back; but he insisted on going on, to prolong the pleasure he felt at taking them both out. 'You can go on if you wish,' Olive said. 'But Gwen will be wanting her tea.' There was a sharpness in the words, a distinct ruffling of feathers, and Mr Stone felt himself heavily rebuked for his thoughtlessness. The incident did not increase his affection for the fat child who was 'wanting her tea'. And tea with Gwen and Olive became an entertainment he dreaded, particularly as in those days Olive was 'living for her child', and facing life with a degree of bravery Mr Stone thought excessive.

At the tea table in Balham, then, he was constrained. There was nothing to constrain Gwen, and Olive herself was fully and happily occupied with Gwen, supplying food as well as the occasional sharp word. (What delight Olive had taken in the food ritual imposed by a government so conscious of Gwen: the milk and orange juice and cod-liver oil beneficently doled out, sacramentally received and administered!) At length, the feeding drawing to a close, his constraint became noticeable and Olive asked him to tell Gwen about the holiday in Ireland from which he had just come back.

He had so far failed miserably in his attempts to amuse Gwen, and he knew that the performance which Olive required would be carefully assessed, for Olive was at the stage where, with the instincts of the school-teacher and the widowed mother forbiddingly allied, she graded people according to their ability to 'get on' with children and with Gwen in particular.

So after the tea things had been cleared away, and Olive had seated herself in her brown-leather armchair (typical of her furniture) and taken out her knitting – how, in her bravery, Olive had tried to age herself! Did he ever see her with knitting needles nowadays? – Mr Stone took Gwen on his lap, and the ordeal began.

Trying to see it all with the eye of a child, he told as

simply as he could of the train journey and the boarding of the great liner. He had a good time giving her an idea of the size of the liner, and he thought he was doing well. Then he came to the first glimpse of Cobh. It had been a misty, drizzling morning, and on a hill of the palest rain-blurred green there had appeared a tall, white building, rising like a castle in a storybook. It was an enchantment which he thought a child might share, and as he spoke he re-lived that moment at dawn on the rainswept deck of the liner, the sea grey and restless, men in oilskins in small, tossing boats, the lines of sea and land and sky all blurred by rain and mist.

'Too self-conscious and namby-pamby,' Olive said at the end.

And there was something in what she said. What he felt now, standing in the dark bathroom, watching the lights of the houses brightening in that period of pause between the activity of day and the activity of evening, was something like what he felt then. Nothing that came out of the heart, nothing that was pure ought to be exposed.

'Well, I think it's a lotta rubbish.'

And of course Margaret was right.

Nothing that was pure ought to be exposed. And now he saw that in that project of the Knights Companion which had contributed so much to his restlessness, the only pure moments, the only true moments were those he had spent in the study, writing out of a feeling whose depth he realized only as he wrote. What he had written was a faint and artificial rendering of that emotion, and the scheme as the Unit had practised it was but a shadow of that shadow. All passion had disappeared. It had taken incidents like the Prisoner of Muswell Hill to remind him, concerned only with administration and success, of the emotion that had gone before. All that he had done, and even the anguish he was feeling now, was a betrayal of that good emotion. All action, all creation was a betrayal of feeling and truth. And in the process of this betrayal his world had come tumbling about him. There remained to him nothing to which he could anchor himself.

In the routine of the office, as in the rhythm of the seasons, he could no longer participate. It all went without reference to himself. Soon it would go on without his presence. His earlier petulance – 'Why do you ask *me*? Why don't you ask Mr Whymper?' At which the ridiculous young man from Yorkshire with the ridiculous clothes had actually sniggered, and reported that 'Pop', the foolish and common nickname which that foolish and common boy had succeeded in popularizing, wasn't in a good mood that morning – his earlier petulance had given way to weariness and indifference and then at last to a distaste for the office which was like fear.

There were days when the office was made unbearable for him by the knowledge that Whymper was present. He felt that Whymper's indifference had turned to contempt, of the sort which follows affection; he thought it conveyed reassessment, rejection and offended disgust. There were times when he felt that he had brought this contempt on himself, that his own revulsion and hostility had been divined by Whymper, who was demonstrating his disregard for the judgement by an exaggerated heartiness with the other members of the staff. He had certainly unbent considerably towards them in these last weeks, and the Whymperish gambit of joviality followed by coldness was less in evidence. 'Tell them a joke,' Whymper used to say in the early days. 'They will laugh. The fresh ones will try to tell you a joke in return. You don't laugh.'

The young accountant had frequently fallen victim to this tactic. Now, fortified by Whymper's friendship – he was Whymper's new lunch companion – he attempted to use it on more junior staff. He also tried to embarrass typists by staring at their foreheads, an 'executive's' gambit which Mr Stone had heard of but had never seen practised. The detestable young man now tapped his cigarettes – it was his affectation to smoke nothing but Lambert and Butler's

Straight Cut, with the striped paper – in the Whymper manner. And – these young men appeared to be having an effect on one another – Whymper came back to the office one afternoon wearing an outrageous bowtie: the junior accountant sometimes wore bowties. Mr Stone could imagine the abrupt decision, the marching off to the shop with the young accountant, the determined yet slack-jawed expression as Whymper bought perhaps half a dozen. Thereafter Whymper always wore bowties; and, since he was Whymper, they were invariably askew. Mr Stone thought they looked a perfectly ridiculous pair of young men, particularly on Saturday mornings, when the young accountant came to work in a 'county' outfit, with a hat far above his station. The hat Mr Stone especially loathed. It was green, with a green feather, as though the boy might at any moment be setting off across the moors.

On calmer days Mr Stone felt that Whymper might only be reacting against his former indiscretions, though he was convinced that these indiscretions and perhaps others were being repeated to the junior accountant. He also saw in Whymper's strange behaviour proof of the now persistent rumour that Whymper was soon going to leave the Unit and might indeed be resigning from Excal.

Altogether, it was a relief when Whymper left for his holiday, though the presence of his familiar never ceased to be irritating.

Margaret appeared to be unusually excited when she let Mr Stone in that evening – such duties no longer being performed by Miss Millington, who had been dismissed with a standing invitation, so far not taken up, to come back and watch television whenever she liked – and it was with an unusually businesslike air that she hustled Mr Stone into the sitting-room. There he found Olive. She was dressed as for a morning's shopping, in clothes formal yet festive. But she looked grave and exhausted, and Margaret wore a careful expression in which concern was mingled with the plain desire not to be thought interfering. With her subdued impresario-like manner Margaret seated Mr Stone, then settled down herself. It was clear that Olive had brought news of importance and that this news – there were cups of tea about – had already been given. But it was not immediately forthcoming, for first there were the inquiries about the office from Margaret and Olive, and there were offers of tea and the things that went with tea. Then, the scene prepared, Margaret glanced at Olive as though encouraging her to begin, and then glanced at Mr Stone, almost, it seemed – Mr Stone couldn't help being reminded of the infants' radio programme – to see whether he was 'comfortable'. She herself sat forward in her chair, restlessly rocking about and rearranging her skirt over her knees as though she had made several witticisms.

At last it came out, and the calmest person appeared to be Olive.

Gwen wanted to go away on holiday with Whymper.

Margaret, watching them both anxiously like a referee, asked, 'Did you know about this, Richard?'

He didn't reply. But his mind, ranging far and fast, instantly settled on various incidents which, though ignored at the time, now turned out to have registered. The deceptions of the young never took in the young; they took in only the old. So much about Whymper's recent behaviour was now explained. The burden of such secrecy had been too great, even for Whymper. And Mr Stone had no doubt that this secrecy had been maintained at the instance of Gwen: he could see the sour foolish face as, mistaking her own fulfilment for power, she childishly exacted promises and made threats in Whymper's shabby front room with the bullfighting poster, Whymper's tenants moving about the hall outside.

But Whymper!

'Well, of course you'll refuse. Gwen's just being very foolish.'

He noted their hesitation.

Then Olive said that Gwen had left home that morning and gone to Whymper's house.

'This is ridiculous. Utterly ridiculous.' He got up and walked about the tigerskin. 'And if you knew what I know about him you wouldn't both be sitting there looking so pleased with yourselves.' They were, in fact, both looking up at him with some apprehension. 'Whymper! Bill! The man is – the man is immoral. I know him better than any of you. Immoral,' he repeated, adding with satisfaction, 'and common. Immoral and common.'

His violence startled them. The saliva in the corners of Olive's mouth was perceptible.

'We are as shocked and upset as you are, Richard,' Margaret said unconvincingly. 'But I don't imagine Olive came here to hear you talk like this.'

'All this talk about a pagan country,' Mr Stone said.

There was a pause.

'Wanting her tea,' he said reflectively. 'Well, she's got it now. Running off with this man just like any shop assistant on holiday. And now you come to see me. Why don't you go to *Bill*? But I imagine you want me to go and bring her home and read her a little Enid Blyton and tell her a little story about what I did at the office today.' He saw himself entering Whymper's house, saw Whymper's frightened, contemptuous face; saw Gwen sulky, satisfied, triumphant; saw Whymper being 'firm' and offensive. It was too much. 'But that's something you and Margaret can see about. *You* can tell her about the big red bus and the choo-choo train.'

'Richard!' Margaret cried. The solemn scene she had visualized was all but destroyed.

Too late, then, it came out that Gwen was pregnant.

'I'm not surprised! I'm not surprised!' He was, deeply. 'But the welfare state hasn't run short of milk and orange juice and cod-liver oil.'

And incapable of further irony, he grew so violent in his language that it was all Margaret could do to prevent an open breach between brother and sister.

It was only later, when Olive had left, with nothing settled or even talked over, that he calmed down.

'I don't understand you, Richard,' Margaret said that evening when they were getting ready for bed. 'If you hate them both so much, why should you be so upset?'

'You are quite right,' he said, looking out of the bedroom window past the old thick brown velvet curtains. 'You are quite right. They deserve one another. And I loathe them both.' He even managed a laugh. 'Poor Olive.'

Before the end of thc week Whymper's resignation was officially announced.

'Bill's had an offer from Gow's,' the junior accountant said importantly. 'Sacred Gow's, the gondemporary people.'

His master's voice, Mr Stone thought.

And on Thursday afternoon the boy came into Mr Stone's office with a copy of the *World's Press News*.

'Have you seen this about Bill?'

Next to a photograph of a presentation of antique furniture to a retiring executive, Mr Stone read:

Bill Whymper Joins Gow's

Bill Whymper is leaving Excal at the end of this month to take up the newly created executive position of publicity director with Gow's. 'The appointment emphasizes the importance attached to progressive marketing and publicity policies in Gow's expanding operations, and Mr Whymper will advise in the overall formulation and rcview of plans,' a spokesman said.

Mr Whymper moves to this top post with the asset of years of success in Excal's P.R. division. He will be remembered as the man behind the energetic and resourceful promotion of Excal's signally successful 'Knights Companion' scheme last year.

When at last he put the paper down, the office was silent. He went out into the corridor. Traffic noises came up from the street unchallenged. The typists' room was empty, lights turned off, the machines all draped with black covers. The clock said twenty past four.

7

London was walking that day. He had forgotten the one-day transport strike which, only partial in the morning, had steadily mounted in drama, the evening papers issuing breathless front-page bulletins on the dislocation and suspension of services. He found the Embankment choked with unmoving cars and buses. People who had stood in hopeless queues and fought to get seats in buses remained where they were and stewed in the heat: the strikers had chosen a fine day. And still, scarcely noticeable in the slow two-way movement on the crowded pavements, the queues remained. At first he stood in a queue. Then he pursued a rogue bus down a side street into the Strand, boarded it without difficulty and discovered it was going no farther. So he decided to walk. And he walked with the city. Along the Embankment, across the bridge, losing all sense of time and distance in the steady tread of thousands of feet, here in the openness of the glinting river crisper and more resonant, he walked with swinging strides, enjoying the exertion, not looking forward to the end, wishing to exhaust himself, to numb the pain within him, hardly aware of the people about him, faceless, their clothes in the mass so uniform, the military-minded and the officerly alone distinguishing themselves by their stride and the little competitive knots about them. Across the river, many disappeared into Waterloo Station, and corner by corner thereafter the noise of feet diminished and the pavement cleared. The signs of commonplace public houses, open doors revealing empty cream-and-brown interiors, were like invitations to rest and relief. And now the walk required will, for it led through long streets of dark brick and stucco peeling like the barks of the pollarded plane trees, past rows of small bright shops made more mean by signboards and display cards and samples bleaching in the windows. Nightly, from the warm, bright heart where they worked and to which they went back for their pleasures, the people of the city returned to such areas, such streets, such houses.

And as he walked through the long, dull streets, as with each step he felt his hips and thighs and calves and toes working, his mood changed, and he had a vision of the city such as he had had once before, at the first dinner party he and Margaret had given. (Gwen was there, and Olive, and Grace and Tony Tomlinson, and Miss Millington had cooked and served her inimitable chips.) He stripped the city of all that was enduring and saw that all that was not flesh was of no importance to man. All that mattered was man's own frailty and corruptibility. The order of the universe, to which he had sought to ally himself, was not his order. So much he had seen before. But now he saw, too, that it was not by creation that man demonstrated his power and defied this hostile order, but by destruction. By damming the river, by destroying the mountain, by so scarring the face of the earth that Nature's attempt to reassert herself became a mockery.

He had now reached Brixton, with its large, glass-fronted shops, its modernistic police station and antique food stalls, its crowds of black and white. Here the walkers were not noticeable. There were long but manageable queues at the bus stops. Several buses arrived; many people got off. He jumped a queue, found himself within the warding-off arm of a conductor on a 109 bus, and rode home. He was grateful for the ride. He was beginning to be fatigued and his breath was failing.

As he walked up the street to his home with long, hard strides, he felt himself grow taller. He walked as the destroyer, as the man who carried the possibility of the earth's destruction within him. Taller and taller he grew, firmer and firmer he walked, past the petty gardens of petty houses where people sought to accommodate themselves to life, past the blank, perceptive faces of cats, past the 'To Let' and 'For Sale' signs, and all the transient handiwork of Eddie and Charley.

At his door he rang. Harder, and longer. The house was empty. Margaret was with Olive and Grace. Happy band of sisters! He fetched out his own key, opened, let himself into the dark hall.

The eyes were green.

Fear blended into guilt, guilt into love.

'Pussy.'

But before the word was fully uttered the young black cat was down the steps, and before any further gesture could be made was out through the open door.

He was no destroyer. Once before the world had collapsed about him. But he had survived. And he had no doubt that in time calm would come to him again. Now he was only very tired. In the empty house he was alone. He took the briefcase up to the study, to wait there and perhaps to do a little work until Margaret arrived.

Srinagar, August 1962

BY THE SAME AUTHOR

A Turn in the South

'An extraordinary panorama . . . anyone who wishes to attempt to understand the problems that still pursue the South should certainly read Mr Naipaul's book' – *Daily Telegraph*. 'A supremely interesting, even poetic glimpse of a part of America foreigners either neglect or patronize' – *Guardian*

The Enigma of Arrival

'It confirms again the truth that he is one of the finest and most penetrating novelists among us' – Bernard Levin in the *Sunday Times*. '*The Enigma of Arrival* newly constitutes Naipaul's claim to be, as a novelist and critic of societies, the most important import since Joseph Conrad and Henry James' – *London Review of Books*

Finding the Centre

'It is now nearly thirty years since . . . on smooth, "non-rustle" BBC script paper, I wrote the first sentence of my first published book . . .' 'Subtle and satisfying' – Martin Amis in the *Observer*

and:

Among the Believers
An Area of Darkness
A Bend in the River
A Flag on the Island
Guerrillas
A House for Mr Biswas
In a Free State
India: A Wounded Civilization
The Loss of El Dorado
The Middle Passage
Miguel Street
The Mimic Men
The Mystic Masseur
The Overcrowded Barracoon
The Return of Eva Perón
The Suffrage of Elvira